Three vivid and entertaining stories about teenagers by Jan Mark, one of the most highly acclaimed writers for young people today.

It's Frankie's seventeenth birthday and, on her day out to celebrate, she buys a crazy hat and plays football. Her younger sister, Sonia, is amazed at Frankie's sudden re-emergence as a carefree teenager from her life as a wife and mother, weighed down by domesticity. Somehow she doesn't feel that Frankie would want her new football team-mates to know that she is somebody's mum . . .

Robert is now a frequent visitor to Yo-Yo's house. He's meant to be her new boyfriend but he seems to spend quite a lot of time with Ben, her younger brother, and with their pet rat, Rat. Whatever is Yo-Yo to think and how soon will everyone around her be wondering too?

When her mother is ill, Ronda volunteers to take over her job – cleaning and looking after the flat of a business-woman, Chloe. Ronda finds out that Chloe is fascinated by the sight of the trains passing beneath her window, and one morning Ronda decides to make the train passengers fascinated by the view of Chloe's flat too . . .

Jan Mark has twice won the Carnegie Medal – for *Thunder and Lightnings* and *Handles*. She was born in Hertfordshire and grew up in Kent. After studying at Canterbury College of Art she taught art in Gravesend. She now lives in Oxford.

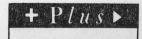

JAN MARK

Frankie's Hat

Illustrated by Quentin Blake

PENGUIN BOOKS

PENGUIN BOOKS

Published by the Penguin Group
27 Wrights Lane, London W8 5TZ, England
Viking Penguin Inc., 40 West 23rd Street, New York, New York 10010, USA
Penguin Books Australia Ltd, Ringwood, Victoria, Australia
Penguin Books Canada Ltd, 2801 John Street, Markham, Ontario, Canada L3R 1B4
Penguin Books (NZ) Ltd, 182–190 Wairau Road, Auckland 10, New Zealand

Penguin Books Ltd, Registered Offices: Harmondsworth, Middlesex, England

First published by Viking Kestrel 1986
Published in Penguin Books 1988

Copyright © Jan Mark, 1986
Illustrations copyright © Quentin Blake, 1986
All rights reserved

Made and printed in Great Britain by
Hazell Watson & Viney Limited
Member of BPCC plc
Aylesbury Bucks
Filmset in Melior

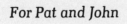

For Pat and John

Contents

Frankie's Hat

Frankie was very nearly late. As the coach turned steeply into the bus station Sonia saw her hurrying across the car park, pushing Simon in his pram, which lurched and bumped over the potholes. A heavy carrier bag of shopping swung from either hand and an economy-size box of washing powder jumped up and down in the tray beneath the pram.

She'll never make it before me, Sonia thought, but the coach became stuck behind a reversing double-decker and in the hooting confusion Frankie, wearing and tacking between buses like a sailing dinghy in a harbour crowded with ocean liners, managed to reach the coach bay first. When Sonia came down the steps she was standing by the timetable, pushing the pram backwards and forwards with little shoves and tugs, and tapping her foot.

'What kept you?' Frankie said. 'I was about to give up and go home.'

'Hah! I saw you,' Sonia said. 'I saw you running in the car park.'

'All that way away? How did you know it was me?'

'You're so little. You do look funny with that pram.'

'I got stuck in the queue in Boots,' Frankie said. 'It's

ever so crowded since they closed that other branch in Queen Street.'

'You should have saved the shopping till after,' Sonia said. 'I could have helped you.'

'You're on holiday,' Frankie said.

'It's only three days.'

'Still a holiday. Aren't you going to say hello to Simon, then?' Frankie gave the pram a nudge with her foot. 'Simon, look who's here.'

Simon was eleven weeks old. He looked at who was there, a long, cool look, and waved a leg, aimlessly.

'Hello, Simon,' Sonia said. She had not met Simon often enough to be at ease with him and felt almost that she had to be polite.

'Say hello to Auntie Sonia,' Frankie said.

Simon ignored them, as if he knew he was too young to be made to do anything and was determined to enjoy the privilege. It would be a long while before anyone could nag him, and he smiled. Sonia felt shy. She was over the excitement of being Simon's auntie. Now it just made her feel strange, as it had done when Frankie had brought Simon to the house and called Mum and Dad 'Granny and Grandpa'. She had looked round, expecting to see her own grandparents.

'Shall we get on home?' Frankie said. 'Or do you want a cup of tea or something?'

'Where?'

'In there, I suppose,' Frankie said, nodding toward the bus station café. Both of her hands were full.

'Let's take something,' Sonia said. 'I can wait till we get back to the flat for tea.'

'No, you've got your own bag. I'm only carrying the stuff because it all spilled out running over those potholes.' Frankie stooped and stacked the carriers on the pram tray. 'Now you can dump your bag on the end, here.'

'Poor old Simon won't have anywhere to put his feet.'

'He usually puts them in his mouth,' Frankie said. 'Hey, Sonia, what have you got in here – bricks?'

'Mum sent some tins,' Sonia said.

'I suppose she thinks we're on our beam ends, as usual,' Frankie said, angrily.

'No – she didn't mean it like that,' Sonia said, but Frankie had turned the pram with an irritable jerk and was heading for St George's Place. 'Shall I push?'

Frankie took no notice. Sonia followed her along the unfamiliar streets and wondered what she had said to make Frankie so annoyed. Surely she could not really be offended because Mum had sent along some tins of fruit and baked beans and stewing steak?

'Anyone'd think Duncan was on the dole,' Frankie said as they galloped up New Inn Hall Street. She was growing more and more angry and the angrier she became the faster she walked. By the time they reached Bonn Square, where the punks and the drunks and the foreign boy scouts were sitting in the sun, Sonia was having to run to keep up, as if she were some kind of a nuisance that Frankie was trying to get away from.

'Oh, calm down, Frankie. *Slow* down. Look, d'you want an ice cream?'

'I can't *afford* ice cream,' Frankie said.

'I can,' Sonia answered unwisely. 'Mum gave me some money –'

'I suppose she thought *I* wouldn't have enough,' Frankie snapped.

'No! It was just for spending.'

'I don't know why she let you come if she thought I couldn't afford to have you here.'

'Oh, please.' On the other side of the street, outside Selfridge's, was a tricycle with an ice cream cart attached to the front of it. A young man in a straw boater was leaning on the cart, waiting for customers. 'Go on, Frankie. Mum only gave me extra because it's a holiday and that.'

'Please yourself,' Frankie said.

'What sort do you want?'

'Anything. I don't care so long as it's cold.'

Sonia bought two Orange Maids and peeled off the wrappers to put in the waste bin. The holiday seemed spoilt almost before it had begun. All around them were tourists and shoppers in summer clothes, people having a good time; on the corner a barrel organ was grinding out lively music and the sun shone. All Frankie could see were crowds and dust. Sonia looked at their reflections in the window of Selfridge's. They were almost the same height and although Frankie was wearing a pink-striped sun-dress and white sandals with high heels, while Sonia was in jeans and a T-shirt, it would have been a very sharp observer who could have guessed that Frankie was seventeen tomorrow and Sonia was twelve last month. Frankie had got married just after she left school, a year ago. Now she had not only a husband, Duncan, but a son, Simon; Sonia's nephew; Mum's grandson. A lot had happened in a year.

They walked up to Carfax, licking the Orange Maids, and found themselves passing through a jam of foreign visitors who, not knowing where to go next, were going nowhere, turning on the spot, shouting, laughing and elbowing each other.

'This place gets worse every year,' Frankie said, plunging ahead with the pram as if it were an ice-breaker.

'You haven't been here a year yet.'

Frankie took no notice. 'It's bad enough in winter, but now . . .!' She caught a tall Frenchman behind the knees with the prow of the pram and he buckled. 'As soon as the University goes down the tourists come up. You'd never think anybody actually *lived* here.'

'Where is the University?' Sonia asked, looking all round. All she could see were shops.

'Where it was last time. All over the place. We'll be passing some of the colleges going down the High Street.'

'I didn't see the town last time,' Sonia said. 'Dad drove round the Ring Road.' When Mrs Arnold had asked her, on the last day of term, where she would be going for her holiday, and she had said 'Oxford', Mrs Arnold, not knowing that it was for only three days, had cried, 'Oh! How marvellous! The city of dreaming spires.' Sonia did not mention that Frankie and Duncan lived in a flat off Cowley Road and that the only spire in the area was on the Presbyterian Church.

The High Street was long and curving. Once they were past the shops and out of the crowds Sonia had time to notice the old buildings that flanked it on either side, and paused to admire them.

'Are they the colleges?'

'Yes; that's University College, that's All Souls, and that one with a sort of summer-house on top is Queen's.'

'They're lovely,' Sonia said, 'better than Buckingham Palace. That's all stone, isn't it – not concrete? It's the colour of honey on bread and butter.'

'Huh, that's just the sunshine. You should see it in the rain,' said Frankie. 'Oh, it is a drag, this walk.'

They crossed Magdalen Bridge beneath the great tower of the college. Sonia wanted to linger and look down into the river, but Frankie stormed on. Sonia followed, feeling that it was all her fault that Frankie had had to walk so far to meet her on a hot day.

'Couldn't you have left Simon with someone and got the bus?'

'Only Susan Powers downstairs, and she's so nosy. Anyway, it's easier for the shopping with the pram.'

'Can't you shop up Cowley Road?'

'Well, you *can*,' Frankie said grudgingly. Sonia gave up trying to look on the bright side and plodded behind.

'It'll be different once we get to the flat,' Sonia kept telling herself. She remembered Frankie in the flat when she last came to visit with Mum and Dad, just before Simon was born. Up till then she had always found it hard to think of Frankie being married, even though she had been her bridesmaid, but when she saw Frankie getting lunch in the kitchen, in her maternity dress, while Duncan put up shelves and got in the way, she had thought, 'Mr and Mrs Osney', and suddenly Frankie had looked like somebody's proper wife and not her sister any more. Mrs Frances Osney. Frankie Osney sounded funny.

The flat was down St Clement's Lane, which sounded to Sonia as if it ought to run between leafy meadows to an old village church. Frankie and Duncan lived on the first floor up an outside concrete staircase. There was a pub opposite and a shop next door that seemed to sell nothing but second-hand car batteries. Frankie went up the stairs backwards, jerking the pram after her one step at a time on its rear wheels.

Inside the front door was a square hall where Frankie parked the pram.

'Shall I unpack?' Sonia asked.

'Just leave everything on the working surface.' Frankie pushed open the kitchen door with her foot. 'You can dump the washing basket on the floor if there's no room. I'm going to change Simon.'

Sonia was going to say, 'What? For a bigger one?' but decided that it would not be a good idea. Frankie did not look as if she would find that kind of joke very funny any more. She carried the bags into the kitchen and began to unpack them. Frankie did not buy the same kinds of things that Mum bought. Lucky Frankie, going shopping with her own money to shops that she had chosen, instead of trailing round Tesco's with a list of things that someone else had written out.

The kitchen, at the back of the building, was cool. Frankie's begonias bloomed on the window sill between the cotton curtains. Sonia remembered how, just before Frankie and Duncan had moved to Oxford, she and Mum and Frankie had gone shopping in Birmingham and come home with parcels of cloth for curtains and cushion covers. Frankie had made everything that could be made herself. She had even covered her own lamp-shades with the bits left over.

When all the shopping was stacked on the working surface Sonia went back to the pram, collected her travelling bag and looked round the door of the spare bedroom. Ske knew it was spare because Frankie's and Duncan's room was the big one at the side, but she had forgotten about Simon. It was Simon's room now, and being so small was two-thirds full with Simon's cot. In the cot was a carry-cot and in the carry-cot was Simon.

Frankie was sidling about in the little bit of space left over, with armfuls of napkins and blankets.

'Where'm I sleeping then?' Sonia asked.

'You can share with me,' Frankie said. 'It's a big enough bed and the sheets were clean on this morning.'

'Where's Duncan, then?' Sonia was shaken. She liked Duncan, even though she hardly ever saw him. When she was bridesmaid at the wedding he had given her a pair of roller skates. A lot of the family had thought that this was a bit odd. 'It's usually a locket or a bangle,' Aunt Julia had said, 'something gold.' But Sonia had wanted the skates for ages and Duncan had taken care to ask her beforehand what she would like, even walking round to Rabson's with her one evening, so that she could point out the right pair in the window. She had been looking forward to seeing him all day, knowing that he came home from work at six o'clock. Where could he be?

'He's gone on a course, that's all,' Frankie said. 'In Sheffield, that's *all*.'

'A course?'

'The firm sent him. I don't know what it's about – I didn't ask.' She crashed shut the bottom drawer of the wardrobe with her heel. 'I mean, Son, he's away for a whole week and it's my birthday tomorrow. He won't even be back for our anniversary.'

'Couldn't he not go?'

'Of *course* he couldn't. It's *work*, isn't it? Look, move

out of the way, will you? I can't get out of the door with you standing around in it like a traffic bollard.' Frankie pushed past and went into the kitchen. 'You might have put the kettle on. Dump your bag on the bed.'

Duncan was older than Frankie and worked in a builder's office. Going on courses was important if he wanted to hang onto his job, but that was no comfort to Frankie, who was going to miss celebrating her birthday and her anniversary because of it.

Sonia threw her bag onto the double bed in the big room and wandered into the kitchen.

'Is that why you asked me over, then?'

'Why?'

'So you'd have someone here on your birthday?'

'Of course it wasn't – I didn't know he was going to be away when I asked you over.'

'Where would I have slept, then?'

'In the lounge. We've got one of those folding beds. What do you take me for?' Frankie snapped.

'Well, I wouldn't have minded,' Sonia said. 'Shall I make the tea?'

'No, I'll do it. Well, *I* mind. We were all going over to Burford Wildlife Park and take lunch and have tea out.'

'Can't we go on the bus?'

'What, with him in a carrier bag?' Frankie demanded, jerking her thumb at the party wall beyond which lay Simon's room.

'We could take the carry-cot and have a handle each.'

'No thanks very much,' said Frankie. 'It'd be just like

shopping only nothing to show for it afterwards.' She grinned suddenly and for a moment Sonia recalled what Frankie had been like once upon a time.

'I'm sorry,' Frankie said, seeing her look. 'I'm being a right old rat-bag, aren't I?'

Once upon a time Sonia would have said, 'Yes,' and they would have a good punch-up, but you could not have a punch-up with a grown-up. She just shook her head and said, 'It's all right.'

Frankie made the tea and they took it into the lounge.

'Just time to drink it before his lordship wants his supper,' said Frankie. Sonia took her cup and leaned back on Frankie's settee, against one of Frankie's cushions. Frankie had decided what kind of a lounge she wanted even before the wedding, and when Duncan found the flat she had gone straight out to make sure that she got it. It was all exactly as she had planned, right down to the glass-topped coffee table and the oatmeal covers on the three-piece suite.

'Don't spill anything on that,' Frankie said, as Sonia set down her cup on the arm of the settee. 'We'll be for ever paying for it.' She switched on the television and they watched *Playschool*.

Sonia looked up sometimes and stared at her sister, and wondered what had happened. Frankie had not grown any taller and did not look any older, but there was a scowl coming between her eyebrows, one short line as if someone had drawn it in sharply and swiftly with a felt-tipped pen.

F.H.—2

At five Frankie fed Simon, then they watched the news, then Frankie said that she would put Simon down. Sonia did not care for the sound of that. Mrs Hitchman, next door, had had the dog put down.

'Can I help bath him?'

'No – I bathed him this morning. I just top and tail him at night.'

This sounded even worse: topped, tailed and put down: but Frankie meant only that she would change him and wash his hands and face. When Simon was tucked into his carry-cot Frankie came back to the kitchen, where Sonia was washing up the tea things.

'I don't suppose you got any lunch.'

'I had a sandwich at the bus station before I came away,' Sonia said. She was beginning to feel really hungry. There had been no cake with the tea, not even biscuits. 'Don't you eat when Duncan comes in?'

'Yes, but he's not coming in, is he?' Frankie said. 'Oh, I'll get something later on. One of those tins Mum sent, and a bit of salad.'

'What happened to the recipe cards?' Sonia asked. Before Frankie was married she had bought a card index and pasted in recipes in alphabetical order. Sonia had helped her and they would sit together on Frankie's bed in the evenings, working out such problems as whether to file Rice Pudding under R or under P: Puddings, Rice. They had had a lot of fun with that card index; it had been like a game. In those days the whole idea of Frankie getting married had been like a game. Helping

Frankie to set up her own home had been like buying a doll's house and furnishing it. When Sonia thought about Frankie in her flat she always saw her standing still, by the stove, in the lounge, on the concrete steps, never walking about; as if she were a doll herself, that had to be picked up and moved into different positions.

'Oh,' said Frankie, 'it's too late to cook anything, isn't it?'

'There were salads on those cards,' Sonia said.

'Who needs a recipe for salad?' Frankie said, and later on they had salad without a recipe: lettuce, tomatoes and beetroot: and without any dressing, either.

Sonia woke next morning feeling sad before she felt strange. For a moment she could not remember where she was, but she knew even before this that she was not feeling happy. Then she turned over to see Frankie asleep beside her and remembered where she was, and why she was unhappy, all at once.

It was only seven o'clock. She did not know when the postman would come and whether or not he would bring birthday cards – the family's gifts and cards were in her bag – but she thought it might cheer Frankie up to be woken with a cup of tea. Simon was still asleep. She had a feeling that he had cried in the night and that Frankie had got up to feed him, but she herself had not woken.

The postman came as she was pouring the tea. Sonia

saw his dark shape loom outside the frosted glass door
and went to open it before he could knock, in case he
had parcels, but he had not. There was nothing for
Frankie and only a buff envelope with a window in it
for Duncan. Sonia put it on the kitchen table. It was the
kind of envelope that was not welcome at home. She
took the rattling tea tray into the bedroom and while
Frankie awoke – not by degrees as she used to do, but
all of a piece, suddenly sitting up – she fetched the
cards and gifts from her travelling bag.

'Happy birthday,' she said, making a little heap of
her offerings on Frankie's lap.

Frankie blinked. 'Wha-a-a-a?' and Sonia saw that she
was still asleep.

'Sorry. I thought you'd woken up. You used to take
ages to come round.'

'Not since I had Simon,' Frankie said, waking properly. 'When he cries in the night I'm out of bed before
I've got my eyes open.'

'Happy birthday,' Sonia said again. She added cau-
tiously, 'All these are from us at home. There wasn't
anything in the post.'

'Oh, Duncan said he left his on top of the wardrobe.
Fetch it down, will you? Nothing else at all – in the
post?'

'Only a bill or something.'

'Huh, we can get those any day. His mum and dad
haven't sent anything, then? Miserable bunch.'

Sonia went to the wardrobe and fetched down Duncan's heavy present. Then she poured the tea. There was no second delivery on Saturdays so she was glad that Duncan's gift felt so substantial.

'Mine's on top.'

'I'll save it till last, then,' Frankie said.

'Why, to be awkward?'

'To keep you in suspense, of course.'

'But *I* know what it is.'

'You don't know if I'll like it or not, though, do you?'

'You'd better,' Sonia said. Frankie had always been sharp, but never sharp enough to sting. Sonia already felt as if she had spent the night in a nettle-bed.

Frankie opened Duncan's present.

'Oh,' said Frankie.

Sonia leaned across to look. 'What is it?' It looked like a saucepan with a pattern of flowers on it, but no handle.

'It's a slow cooker with an odour-filter in the lid,' Frankie said, reading from the instruction leaflet.

'Didn't you want one, then?'

'About as much as I want a new lavatory brush,' Frankie said. 'It's my fault. I was moaning to Duncan the other day about cooking smells getting into the lounge. Kitchen door doesn't fit properly, see? Now he's got me this.'

'It must have cost a lot.'

'Yes,' Frankie said. 'It would have been cheaper to mend the door.'

Sonia moved the slow cooker to the end of the bed

while Frankie opened her next present, from Mum and Dad.

'Oh, lovely,' Frankie said, without enthusiasm. Mum's present was a box of place mats with pictures on them of famous London landmarks. Dad had sent a wooden tray that he had made himself, with beautiful brass handles. Mum had suggested that Sonia embroider a tray cloth to go with it, even though Sonia's embroidery usually looked as if it had been done with fuse wire and a screwdriver. Sonia was very relieved that she had refused and had chosen Frankie's present herself. Suddenly things for the flat did not seem to make very exciting presents; all the fun had been in choosing them. It was not like furnishing a doll's house after all.

'This is light,' Frankie was remarking, weighing Sonia's present in her hand. 'What is it, a pot scourer?'

'Try again.'

'A butter-dish cosy?'

'No.' What a good thing it *wasn't* a tray cloth.

Frankie unwrapped it. Inside the fancy paper was a curled white ostrich feather.

'What's this for, then?' Frankie demanded, suspiciously. 'Not for dusting, is it?'

'Not for anything,' Sonia said. 'I just thought you'd like it. You can hang it on the wall, or something. Put it in a vase. You used to like pinning daft things up on the wall.'

'Used to is right,' said Frankie. Then she leaned over

surprisingly and kissed Sonia on the cheek. 'Don't take any notice of me, love. I like it. It's just what I want.'

In the next room, Simon began to yell.

After breakfast Sonia offered to bath Simon. Frankie declined.

'Oh, go on. I'll be ever so careful.'

'It's not a treat, you know.'

'It would be for me.'

'It'd be more of a treat for me if you'd wash up,' Frankie said. She looked tired already, at only half past eight.

While they were both busy the doorbell rang. Sonia went to answer it and found Duncan's sister Bridget on the top of the concrete steps. She had met Bridget only once before, at the wedding, but she recognized her immediately. She was twenty-four, a year older than Duncan, and she looked it, looked grown-up, not, like Frankie, just playing at it.

'Special delivery,' Bridget said, holding up a carrier bag. 'Hello, Sonia, where's your sister? Where's old Dunc?'

'Who *is* it?' Frankie yelled from the bathroom.

' 'Sme. I brought your presies,' Bridget called, and bounced into the hall. Frankie came out of the bathroom with Simon wrapped in a towel. Bridget, who was not married and had no children, seized him. 'Come to Auntie, then. Here, Frankie, what have you done with my little brother?'

27

'He's off on a course, isn't he?' Frankie said.

'On your birthday? Rotten so-and-so. What do you think, Simon?' She held the baby up to face her. 'Isn't your dad a rotten old so-and-so?'

'He couldn't help it,' Frankie mumbled. 'Oh, shut the door, Son.' Simon began to grizzle.

'You don't half look miserable, you lot,' Bridget complained. 'What shall we do to cheer you up? I know, let's go to a funeral. You'd like that, wouldn't you, Simon? They were digging a new grave as I came past the cemetery.'

'Oh, shut up,' Frankie said, but she began to smile. So did Sonia. 'Go and put the kettle on, Son.'

Bridget brought Simon's clothes into the kitchen and dressed him expertly while Sonia made coffee and Frankie opened the presents from Duncan's family. Sonia groaned inwardly. There was a pop-up toaster from his mum and dad, an omelette pan – a very nice non-stick one – from his gran, and a set of cork coasters from his younger brother.

'I think they're all afraid you might get out of the house for a bit,' Bridget said, looking at the presents and then at Frankie's face. She reached into her bag and brought out an envelope. 'This is from me.'

'Milk tokens?' said Frankie, and opened the envelope. Inside was a ten-pound note.

'Go on the town,' Bridget said.

Frankie rubbed her eyes. 'Oh, Brid, you shouldn't have.'

'I know,' Bridget said cheerfully, 'but why not, eh? Look, I've got an idea. I was going to suggest you and Dunc took yourselves out with that, but he's not here. Why don't you go out with Sonia?'

Frankie looked at Simon.

'And I'll stay here and baby-sit. Go on, why not? Stay out all day. We'll be OK, won't we, Simon?'

'You don't mean it?'

'You get going before I change my mind,' Bridget said. 'Go on, jump! I'll finish the washing up.'

Frankie was out of the kitchen and into the bedroom in one bound, dragging Sonia behind her.

'Where are we going?' Sonia said.

'I don't know. It doesn't matter. Out,' said Frankie. She looked at Sonia. 'Here, Son, I wonder if I could still get into your jeans.'

'But I didn't bring anything else,' Sonia said.

'I'll lend you something – anything,' Frankie said. 'Look, you can choose what you like.'

'Haven't you got any jeans now?' Sonia said.

'The last pair split all down the leg. Oh, go on, Son. I haven't worn jeans for *ages*.'

'Can I have that pink sun-dress with the shoulder straps?' Sonia asked, looking in the wardrobe.

'It'll be a bit long on you.'

'Long skirts are in.'

'Well . . . I . . . well . . . *yes*,' Frankie cried. 'You can borrow my sandals, too. The ones with heels. I'll wear your trainers. Come on, Son, let's have those jeans.'

They exchanged clothes and shoes and stood side by side to look in the glass.

'Could be twins,' said Bridget from the doorway, 'only Son looks older.'

'Shove off,' said Frankie, but she looked pleased all the same.

They walked down Cowley Road, round the Plain where the drinking fountain stood inaccessibly in the middle of the road, and onto Magdalen Bridge. Sonia's heels clicked on the pavement and Frankie padded in Sonia's trainers, fanning herself with the ostrich feather. On the bridge Frankie leaned over the balustrade and looked down to the meadow below.

'D'you remember that bridge at home, Son?'

'Of course I do,' said Sonia. 'It's still there. I came over it yesterday morning.'

'D'you remember how we used to run along the top of it?'

'Still do,' Sonia said. She looked at Frankie and saw what Frankie was thinking. 'But that's only a little one. Hey, no – Frankie! It's *miles* down. And it's not even flat on top.'

But Frankie was already scrambling up onto the parapet. 'You can catch me if I fall.'

'Fat chance,' Sonia said. 'If you fall you go down on your own. I'm not with you.'

Frankie took no notice and pranced all the way across the bridge balanced on the parapet and waving the ostrich feather. Sonia refused to look. She was really frightened, and cross. She saw herself going back to the flat alone and trying to explain that Frankie had fallen off Magdalen Bridge.

At the end of the balustrade Frankie jumped down and landed lightly.

'I used to be good at gymnastics, didn't I?'

'Yes,' Sonia said. '*At school*,' she added, pointedly.

'You wouldn't think that I had a baby not three months ago, would you?' Frankie sounded complacent. Sonia said nothing and they walked on up the High Street.

On the far side of the road was a second-hand shop.

'Hang about,' Frankie said. 'I want to look in there.' Sonia glanced across at the glum window filled with dingy garments.

'Oh, Frankie, you're not going to buy clothes in there?'

'Why not?'

'Mum'd have a fit.'

'It's none of her business.' Frankie darted into the roadway among the traffic and left Sonia to follow.

Seen close to the clothes looked even worse, as if they must have been left behind by people who had died and had spent their last years going to funerals. On the floor lay pairs of ugly shoes that seemed to have been designed for ladies with two left feet, or six toes, or hooves.

'You're never going to buy *those*,' Sonia protested,

but Frankie had pushed open the door so she had to go in too or be left outside on the pavement, feeling depressed about the shoes.

Something inside must have caught Frankie's eye, for she went straight to the back of the shop where there was a tall rack with hats displayed on it.

'Oh, Frankie, not one of *them*,' Sonia cried, looking at the knitted tea cosies, felt plant pots and raffia waste-paper baskets. 'Anyway, you don't wear hats.'

'Only because I haven't got any.'

'But not a hat like that. Look, you've got that tenner from Brid —'

'Yes, and you could spend it all on one hat down the Westgate, in Selfridge's. Look, some of these are only 50p.'

'I wouldn't give 50p for the lot,' Sonia said, but Frankie was on her toes and reaching down the topmost hat of all. In a way it was the worst because at least the others were quite small, but this one was clean and fairly new. The straw was still straw-coloured, and the band inside was not marked with unappetizing stains. The only trouble was that it measured about two feet across. When Frankie tried it on, it flapped.

'Looks good, doesn't it?' Frankie peered into a spotty mirror (£2·50).

'No,' said Sonia, but the hat made a successful frame for Frankie's sharp little face.

'I'll have this,' she said to the assistant, who was watching them with suspicion. Cheek, thought Sonia resentfully. If she went shoplifting she would choose somewhere more entertaining than this. 'Hang about, though,' Frankie said. 'I want something to go round it.'

Over a clothes horse (£3·75) hung belts, beads and scarves. Frankie riffled through them and came up with a length of green chiffon with a frayed end.

'What do you think?'

'I think it looks like someone's been chewing it,' Sonia said, 'but that won't stop you, will it?'

'No,' said Frankie, and paid for the scarf and the hat. The scarf cost only ten pence, Sonia was glad to note.

Outside in the street Frankie perched on a window ledge and knotted the scarf round the crown of the hat so that the tails hung down behind. Then she took the ostrich feather and threaded the quill through the straw. It reared up at one side in a cockade and she jammed the hat on her head.

'Always wanted one like this,' Frankie said, gazing at her reflection in the shop window behind her.

'Why didn't you have one, then?'

'Like you said, Mum'd've had a fit. So would Dunc. Couldn't afford it, anyway.' Frankie walked on, giggling.

'I'm not with you!' Sonia called after her.

As they moved up the High Street among the colleges, they began to run into tourists. The tourists looked just like English people, wearing the same kinds of clothes, but you could tell that they were tourists because they went about in clumps. Sonia heard the words, '*Ah, quel chapeau!*' from inside a group of French teenagers and knew that they were talking about Frankie's hat.

'Tell you what this needs,' Frankie said, raising her hand to the brim, 'a flower – one of those false ones. I wish they hadn't closed Woollies.'

'Closed it?' Sonia said.

'Yes, ages ago. I went in on the last day. All the lights were out and the escalators had gone. It was like the end of the world. People were wandering about looking sort of lost – you know: "Woolworth's is closing. What shall we do?" It's a shopping centre, now.'

'You can buy flowers in florists,' Sonia said. 'If you must.'

'Oh, I don't want a real one,' Frankie said. 'In this heat? It'd be all wilted in ten minutes.'

'I know. I meant false ones.'

'In a florist? I wouldn't know.' Frankie stuck out her lower lip. 'I haven't been in a florist's in yonks. Flowers cost the earth. You can't eat flowers.' She brightened. 'There's a florist's in the market. Come on.'

They turned sharp right, into an arcade.

'Is this the shopping centre?'

'No, the covered market. It isn't half a rip-off. People come in here because they think markets are cheap, but you pay through the nose all right, I tell you. Pity it's not Wednesday. There's a real market in the bus station car park – real bargains.'

'Hah! Bargains!' Sonia muttered. 'Catch me buying a second-hand hat.'

'Second-*head* hat,' said Frankie.

The florist, as Sonia had predicted, sold not only artificial flowers but also dried real ones. Frankie chose a silk begonia which looked very nearly real because begonias look artificial in any case, a bunch of grasses, dyed red, and a strange brown thing with holes in it that the assistant said was a lotus head. She gave Frankie's hat a very odd look and was still staring through the window when they stopped outside, where Frankie arranged her purchases round the crown, under the scarf.

'Looks like a garden,' Sonia said. 'All you want's a concrete gnome.'

The market seemed cool under its high roof. When they came out again into Market Street the sun struck them like a bomb blast.

'I wish we were in the country,' Frankie said, discontentedly. 'It's like walking on a hot-plate.'

'Well, we can get a bus, can't we? There's lots of country round here, isn't there? I saw it.'

'It'll be just as hot, though.' Frankie suddenly sat down on the pavement against the wall of the Co-op.

'You can't sit there.'

'Who says? I don't see any signs — *Sitting limited to twenty minutes in any hour.*' Frankie began to take off her shoes.

'What are you *doing*?'

'Taking my shoes off.'

'In the street?'

'Looks like it.'

'I suppose you're going to chuck them in a litter bin,' Sonia complained. 'They're my shoes, remember.'

Frankie tied the laces together and slung the trainers round her neck. 'Tell you what,' she said, 'let's go down the river.'

'What?' Sonia looked dubious. 'Back to Magdalen?'

'No, not *that* river. That's only a little one – the Cherwell. Let's go down the Thames.'

Sonia had seen the Thames before. 'I thought it was in London.'

'Some of it is. It's a river, you know. Not a pond. Goes on for miles. This is the other end.'

'You're not walking through Oxford like that?' Sonia said, looking from Frankie's hat down to her bare feet. 'You look like Huckleberry Finn.'

'It's the Thames, not the Mississippi,' Frankie said.

'This is Folly Bridge.'

'Why Folly?'

'Dunno. Maybe they thought it was a daft place to build a bridge,' Frankie said. 'Oh look, one of those ice cream trikes. D'you want one?'

'You've changed your tune,' Sonia said.

'Well, we're in the money, now, aren't we?' Frankie said, and to prove it bought two Cornettos.

'It's not like the Thames in London, is it?' Sonia said, looking at the river that ran between lime trees, heavy with flowers.

'No – still, I wouldn't like to fall in it, though,' Frankie said.

'There's people swimming over there.'

'Tourists, I bet. I'd just as soon swim in the sewage works, myself,' Frankie said. 'I know, we can walk up as far as Iffley Lock, and get some chips or something, and come back down Iffley Road. Get a bus, even.'

'Chips!' Sonia said. 'In this weather?'

'Maybe they've got a sandwich bar or something. Pity we can't go in a pub.'

'You're old enough.'

'But not to buy intoxicating liquors.'

'We wouldn't want intoxicating liquors.'

'No, but a lot of pubs won't even let you in if you're under eighteen. I have enough trouble when I'm out with Dunc – people won't even believe I'm seventeen. I'd never get away with it today.'

'Well, you're *not* seventeen yet. Not till half past three.' Sonia looked at her sister. In Sonia's jeans, with the legs rolled up, barefoot and crowned with the preposterous hat, Frankie seemed no particular age at all. She could see why Bridget had thought they looked like twins.

Down river the path widened out into a flat grassy space and in a backwater more people were swimming.

'That's Long Bridges Bathing Place,' Frankie said. 'I don't know, though, it looks about as yukky as the river.'

Some boys were playing football. As Frankie and Sonia walked by, the ball went wide and came toward them, heading for the water. Frankie side-stepped, blocked it with her foot and kicked it back. The nearest boy returned it. Sonia thought, personally, that he had done it by accident, but Frankie was on to it in a second.

'Hang about!' Frankie yelled. 'Wait till I get my shoes on.' She put one foot on the ball, to make sure that they did wait, and unslung the trainers. 'Here, Son, hold my hat.'

Sonia was left clutching it as Frankie dived off, dribbling the ball. She had forgotten how fast Frankie was on her feet, how Frankie had once spent all her evenings out on the waste ground behind the house, playing football, how Frankie had once made the front page of the local paper because she had wanted to play in the school eleven and the top brass had said no. The story might have made the national press had not Frankie broken a toe kicking a brick home from school, and by the time it healed the season was over. When Autumn came round again she had stopped playing soccer with the lads and had started marking them in discos instead.

Frankie had lost none of her skill; she was everywhere, dodging, blocking, tackling. One of the boys flopped down on the grass near to where Sonia was standing.

'Want to join in?' he said. 'You can substitute.'

'I'm holding the hat,' Sonia said.

'She your sister?'

'Yes.'

'D'you live round here?'

'No,' Sonia said, truthfully, since *she* did not. 'Balsall Heath.'

'Where's that?'

'Birmingham.'

'You on holiday?'

'Yes.' Well, she was.

'Pity.' The boy looked toward Frankie's high-speed feet. 'We're getting up this five-a-side and the girls keep slagging us because it's all boys and we said, well, if any of them could play decent it'd be different. We could do with your sister, though.'

'Shame,' Sonia agreed. The boy got up and joined the game again, much to her relief. She had managed to avoid telling any untruths, so far, and she did not want to be manoeuvred into lying about Frankie's age, or what she did. She did not think that Frankie would want her new team-mates to know that she was somebody's mum.

When the game had ended they walked on up to Iffley Lock, collecting a swan's feather and two crow's feathers for the hat, also a carrot with its fern still on, that must have dropped out of someone's shopping basket.

Frankie poked it in on the other side from the ostrich feather and the two plumes, the green and the white, nodded at each other across the crown. Frankie had also stuck some lollie sticks into it that she had picked up at intervals along the bank. Sonia thought that was really disgusting.

They had just crossed the river at Iffley Lock and stopped to watch a boat go through, when Frankie saw something bobbing about in the water, almost under the bank.

'What's that, Son?'

'Looks like a baby's rattle,' Sonia said.

'Well, so long as there's no baby on the end of it,' Frankie said, and knelt down to hook it in.

'What d'you want a rattle for?' Sonia said. 'You're never going to give it to Simon – not after it's been in there? Oh, Frankie. *Frankie!*'

A small wind had blown up during the morning. As Frankie leaned over the water a brief gust of it slid under the brim of her hat, lifted it gently from her head and as gently dropped it in the river, a few feet away. It immediately began to move briskly downstream, twirling slightly, like a festive hovercraft.

'Oh, Son,' Frankie wailed. 'Oh no, oh! My hat!'

'It's going to London,' Sonia said, unsympathetically. 'Best place for it.'

'It blooming well isn't,' Frankie said. She stood up, took off the trainers again, scooped the change from

Bridget's tenner out of her back pocket and handed it to Sonia.

Sonia took it, dumbstruck.

'Thanks,' said Frankie, and jumped into the Thames.

'Now she'll drown,' Sonia thought, although Frankie could swim perfectly well. But it would be just her luck if Frankie *did* drown, while she had to go back and tell Bridget and Duncan. People's mothers shouldn't do things like this. Frankie, however, had no intention of drowning. She grabbed the hat and, holding the brim in her teeth, steered it back to shore. Sonia took it and Frankie hauled herself up onto the bank.

'You nutter!' Sonia shouted. 'You idiot! You loony!'

Frankie retrieved the hat and planted it on her dripping hair, but not before she had stuck the rattle, the cause of the incident, into the scarf.

'Good thing it landed right way up,' she said. 'Come on, let's get moving.'

'What?' Sonia cried. 'Moving where? You can't go home like that.'

'Can't stay here, can we?' Frankie said.

'But in the street?'

'I'll dry off as I go.'

'But don't you feel horrible?'

'No. I just feel nice and cool, right now,' Frankie said, 'but I expect I'll start feeling horrible quite soon. So, like I said, let's get moving.'

*

Even Frankie did not have the nerve to insist that

they should go shopping in Iffley after this, but there was no question of getting on a bus, either, so they had to walk back down the Iffley Road with Frankie dripping and steaming at every step, eating Cornish pasties that Sonia had bought from a bakery in the shopping parade.

'Oh,' Frankie said, as they turned into St Clement's Lane. 'I hope Brid's in. I never brought my keys.'

'Just as well,' Sonia said. 'They'd be at the bottom of the Thames by now.'

Fortunately Bridget was in; they could hear Simon yelling before they reached the foot of the concrete steps.

'You're back early,' she said, when she opened the door. Then she took a closer look at Frankie and at what Frankie was wearing. 'What happened to you?'

'Jumped into the Thames after my hat, didn't I?'

'Hat? That?' Bridget gaped. 'It looks like a compost heap.'

'You watch it, young Brid,' Frankie said. She tossed the hat on a chair in the lounge. 'Here, what's the matter with my son, then? What have you been doing to him, Brid? Cutting bits off for lunch?' She rushed into the bedroom and scooped up Simon from his carry-cot.

'Good thing you took your titfer off,' Bridget yelled after her. 'You'd have frightened him into fits.'

Sonia went after Frankie. 'I'll have to keep this dress on now,' she said, 'won't I? You are going to wash my things, aren't you?'

'What do you take me for?' Frankie said. 'Of course I will.'

'I don't know what to take you for,' Sonia complained. Frankie took no notice and addressed herself to Simon. 'What's the matter, then? Did Mummy leave you, then? Did your rotten old mum leave you with nasty Auntie Bridget? Did she, then?'

'There's gratitude,' said Bridget, to Sonia. 'Did you have a good time?'

'She did.'

'Looks like it.'

'Here, go to your Auntie Son,' Frankie said, holding out the baby. Sonia took him. 'I'm going to get changed. Give us those sandals, Son.'

While Frankie was in the bathroom changing her clothes and washing the Thames out of her hair, there was the sound of a key in the lock of the front door and a man's voice called, 'Frankie!'

Sonia and Bridget jumped, but Frankie yelled, 'Duncan!' and rushed out of the bathroom with her hair wrapped in a towel. 'What are you doing here?'

'They cancelled the course, didn't they?' Duncan said.

'Why didn't they tell you before you went?'

'They said there was a letter. I suppose it came after I went.' He grabbed Frankie and swung her round in a hug, grinning over her head at Bridget and Sonia. 'Hello, girls. Make us a coffee then, one of you, eh?'

'Why didn't you come back last night?' Frankie demanded.

'After driving all the way to Sheffield?' Duncan said. 'Have a heart. Anyway, the car'd never have stood it.'

'I'll just finish my hair,' Frankie said, 'and I'll be with you.' She started toward the bathroom. Bridget went into the kitchen. Duncan caught sight of the hat, lying on a chair.

'What in heck is that?'

Frankie looked back round the door.

'Oh, just some old rubbish of Sonia's.'

Sonia opened her mouth, then realized that it might be wisest if she said nothing, so she kissed Simon instead, and said nothing.

Like It Is Round Here

It was a normal morning: my mother was having a row with the rat. Ben (my brother) was cleaning him out and Mum had noticed carrot scrapings among the sawdust.

'He doesn't like the skins,' Ben explained.

'What do you mean, he doesn't like the skins? He's a rat, isn't he?' said my mother. She put her head down close to the aquarium. 'Listen,' she said, 'people like you live in sewers. They eat insulating tape.'

I admit, he's abnormally fussy for a rat, but he's very clean with it. If the cat was half as clean we wouldn't complain. There is no water in the aquarium – he isn't a water rat – but it makes a very good cage. Dad put together a sort of rat-run out of bits from a box the wine came in. It has several levels inside and we call it his multi-storey car park. Rat just looked at Mum and went back into the multi-storey and we could hear him making improvements. He had eaten a great deal of it; funny about the carrot skins.

His kennel name is Ratcliffe Highway but we call him Rat, rather like God is just God. Ben was going to name him Frederick after a friend of my mother's, but Frederick happened to come round the night after he arrived and although he was very polite to him and even stroked him, you could see that it wasn't love at first sight and never would be, even at tenth sight, so that idea got shelved.

We soon found out that introducing people to Rat was a good way of discovering their true feelings, however hard they tried. Robert thought Rat was brilliant and spent ages with Ben, entertaining him. That should have told me a lot about Robert – well, it did, but not the main thing. Still, that morning, Robert was just someone at school. I'd never even spoken to him.

Ben finished mucking out Rat, gave him a scraped carrot ('Dear God,' said Mum, 'you'll be cooking them in butter for him next.') and went off to school. He's still at the Middle School and they start earlier than us. They come home earlier too, because there aren't enough school coaches to go round. I stopped to have a talk with Rat and let him climb on my hand. He sits on your palm and wraps his arms round your thumb. I don't think he notices the rest of us, just our hands, which are his dear old mates. His greatest friend is my father's moustache. He spends a lot of time preening it, as if he hopes that one day it will respond. It might even turn out to be a lady moustache. He's a very manly rat.

I said to Mum, 'Can I ring Mitts before I go?' and she said, 'What on earth for? You'll be seeing her in half an hour.'

I said, 'I want to see if it's all right us going round hers after school.'

Mum said, 'So why not ask her when you see her?'

I said, 'Well, if I ring her now I can tell you whether I'll be late or not. If I wait till I get to school I'll have to ring you from the pay phone. It'll save money, this way.'

'Yeah, your money,' said Mum.

'Oh no,' I said. 'I'd reverse the charges.'

'You're a proper sponge,' said Mum, but she waved me to the phone. She doesn't really mind me phoning people except Sally Cossey who used to live down our lane but moved to Birkenhead. When I ring Cossey she lets me have ten minutes and then picks up the receiver on the extension and pretends to be the speaking clock. She drops really heavy hints, Mum does.

Anyway, I rang Mitts (Sarah Glover – Gloves – Mittens – Mitts. Geddit? Daft) and got her mother, who was in a snot as usual.

'Won't you be seeing her in a little while?' she goes.

I lied. 'I just wanted to ask her about when our history assignment's got to be in,' I said. I didn't want to say anything about going round there that evening in case Mrs G had other ideas. Mitt's mother isn't the kind of person to have ideas of any sort, come to think of it, but she knows how to say no. That's mostly all she does say, which is probably why she is so good at it. Initiative-wise she's a long way behind Rat.

I can imagine what would happen if we introduced Rat to Mrs Glover. Actually, Mitts isn't too hooked on him, either, though so far Karen Hales is the only one who's screamed. Out loud, that is.

'I think she's already left,' says Mrs G.

'Could you just see, please,' I said, all crawly.

'Won't you be late?' she goes, but I heard her put the receiver down and go off hollering 'Sarahrrrr!'

Probably I would be late. It's nearly three miles to school. Ben and I cycle, which is all right except in bad weather, but the lanes are dangerous when the cow parsley's high and you can't see round corners, or at harvest time when the combines are out or when they're lifting sugar beet and there's mud up to the wheel-hubs. When we were at the little school they kept shovelling Green Cross Codes at us, to make us safe on the roads, but they were all about pedestrian crossings and not running out between parked cars; nothing on what to do if you meet Charlie Hemp's combine harvester coming the other way or you get zonked on the head by a falling sugar beet when a lorry belts past. A few drop off on corners. There's always a cairn of sugar beet at the church crossroads, for instance, by the middle of January. They come off in *exactly* the same place.

Put like that, I suppose, it's safe about one day in ten, on average. People think city streets are dangerous, but I've never been hit by a sugar beet in Norwich.

All this time Mrs Glover was Sarahring round the building. It's only a council house but you'd think it was the size of County Hall the way she was yodelling. I reckoned that if Mitts *had* left already she'd hear and come back. Anyway, after a bit Mitts picked up the phone and said 'Yes?'

I said, 'It's me,' so she goes 'Who?' and I go 'Knock knock,' and she goes 'Oh, stop mucking about. I'm late.' She has further to go than me, up the by-pass.

I said, 'It's me. Yo-yo. (Josephine – Jo – Jo-jo – Yo-yo. Worse.) Are we coming round yours tonight?'

She lowered her voice then and sort of muttered. 'Yes. Straight after school. Mum's going to Cromer with my Nan.' She didn't want her mum to hear, I knew. I don't know why. All it is, some of us go round someone's for coffee sometimes, and just talk. Mrs G, and some other mothers too, seem to think we might have an orgy, or worse, start dancing. She thinks I'm a bad influence because I henna my hair and that Mum's worse because she lets me. Sometimes she helps me too, but don't tell Mrs Glover. I think I may be allergic to the dye because I got a lot of big zits round the back of my neck, but it's not going to affect my exam results, is it? It certainly isn't going to affect anyone else's exam results. If Mitts fails everything it'll be because she's thick and bone idle, not because I'm leading her astray.

'Hey,' says Mitts, still on the phone, in spite of being late. 'Emma says Carrow's got a message for you,' and she giggles. That didn't mean it was meant to be funny. Her giggles are sort of punctuation marks, like commas. They give her time to think what's coming next.

'What is it?' I said.

'I can't tell you,' says Mitts, giggle giggle. 'I don't

know what it is, do I? It's not *from* Carrow. Someone gave it to him.'

'Who did?'

'He'll tell you,' says Mitts. 'See you,' and hangs up.

I don't know why I go round with Mitts, really. Every time I hear her voice I want to bang her over the head. She's got lovely hair, though; really really blonde.

Only there's not much under it.

'All fixed up?' Mum said, lurking.

'Yes. I will be late tonight. Home at six.'

'My God, what an exciting life you lead,' said Mum. That was rotten of her. I mean, it's all right to be going on with. I'm not going to live here for ever, after all. (No *way* am I going to live here for ever.) I can wait. *She's* a lecturer in Education at the University, which can't be much more exciting if Frederick's anything to go by: teaching people to be teachers. You'd never think that anyone had ever taught our lot anything, I mean, you'd think they'd have got like that on their own.

I went off to school then. The cow parsley season was just beginning, dead hazardous, but quite pretty, with patches of red campion among all that white lace. As I went down our lane I could see the school coach from Hoxenham, going along the top road, so I had to step on it. They're really in the sticks out at Hoxenham. At least we can get a service bus to Norwich three times a day. Not many people do though. Yarmouth's about as far as anyone goes round here. Really adventurous.

I had to take it fairly slow on account of the cow

parsley, so I was only just in time for assembly and there was no chance to pick up my message from John Carrow. That isn't to say we can't talk in assembly (well, of course, we can't but we *do*), it's just that the boys stand on one side of the hall and the girls on the other. There's no rule about it, it just happens. I suppose there must have been a rule about it once, left over from the days when there were separate entrances for each sex (and we still can't work out who the third door was for), but when it got repealed, nobody took any notice. I was in the middle of our row, and Mitts next door but two, but I had Marie Candell next to me, teacher's lick, and she wouldn't pass any messages on, no way, so I had to wait for first period before I could find out what was going on.

'I don't know what it is,' Mitts kept saying, giggle giggle. 'Carrow just told Emma to tell you to look out for him at break.'

'Well, didn't he say anything what it was about?'

'She didn't say. Wouldn't tell *me*,' says Mitts.

'So why did he say anything to Emma in the first place?' I said, and Mitts giggles.

'I expect he wanted her to prepare you. I expect he knows you're mates.'

'So why did she tell you?'

'Because *we*'re mates,' says Mitts.

'Prepare me for what?' I said. 'Someone died?'

She hadn't thought of that. 'Oh no,' she goes. 'She was smiling.'

'Could be Hopgood's dead, then.' (PE Master.)

I had a horrible thought that maybe Carrow wanted me to go out with him. Not that I don't like old Carrow, he's all right, he's *nice*, but not to go out with. Anyway, you have to be careful who you go out with here; people sort of vet each other. There was this kid in the Third Year, Ian Scott, who said he fancied me, and I liked him and you'd never have known he was only a Third Year, but all the rest of our lot said, 'Ooooh, you can't go out with *him*.' Emma called him a fliddy little wimp. They didn't actually forbid it, but I knew they'd never let up about it. I *was* sorry. I liked him.

Mum did her nut about that.

'For crying out loud,' she said, 'if you like the guy, go out with him.'

'You don't know what it's like,' I said.

'Are you always going to follow the herd?' she said. 'If you must be a sheep, at least be the front sheep.'

She's always on about not following the herd. She hasn't seen the herd. The Fifth Year duff you up if you get too far out of line.

I managed to see Carrow at break, and I even had to plan that like we were secret agents. I saw him *sort of* strolling along the edge of the field, so I had to *sort of* nip round the front of the building, which is out of bounds, and *sort of* run into him by accident, coming the other way. Even then Marie and Emma and Lisa and Mitts and all of them were *sort of* in the same place at the same time, just a few yards behind.

(That's what comes of being front sheep, Mum.)

Carrow goes, 'Oh, I've got a message for you, Yo-yo,' and I go, 'I did hear something about it.'

He goes, 'You know Robert Clarke?'

I knew the name. I couldn't put a face to it.

'In 4J,' says Carrow, and then I knew who he meant. But you hardly talk to anyone out of your own class (let alone your own year), like I said.

'What's he done?'

'He hasn't done anything yet,' says Carrow, 'but he was talking about you yesterday.'

I said, 'Cheek,' because that's what you do have to say, even if you don't think it. I didn't think it, but it felt funny. I mean, our lot talk about each other all the time, so I'm used to that, but here was someone I didn't even know, talking about me. It did feel funny.

'What did he say?' I said.

'He said he thinks you're nice,' Carrow said.

I said, 'Well, I am nice. What else?'

Carrow said, 'He said he thought you'd be a lot of fun to go out with.'

'I expect I would be,' I said, but carefully, in case old Carrow was getting ideas after all.

'He said he wondered if it would be all right to ask you.'

I had to think about that because if I said it was all right for him to ask, it really meant that I was going to say yes if he did ask. I tried to remember if there was anything I'd heard about him that I didn't like, but there wasn't, and I'd never seen him do anything I didn't approve of. He didn't beat up First Years, or go round smashing things, and he wasn't part of the Drugs Problem.

(The teachers are always on about the Drugs Problem, like they were afraid we might not hear about it otherwise. We get talks and films and pamphlets in the library, but it's no good. Nobody takes anything. Actually, we did have a Drugs Problem once, but he left last year and got nicked for something quite different about three months ago. He was his own problem, really.)

'What shall I tell him?' Carrow says, and I noticed we'd walked all the way down to the cricket nets without saying anything, while I was thinking. When we turned round to walk back, there was Mitts, Lisa, Emma and Marie and some of the others, *casually* coming along towards us, all in a bunch. They must have been following us before we turned round and there would only be about thirty seconds before we all ran into each other so I had to act fast.

'Tell him OK,' I said. 'Any time.'

'You sure?' says the idiot Carrow. I wondered why he thought I wouldn't be. Still, I hadn't been, had I?

Then up comes the crowd.

'What's all that about?' says Mitts, loudly. They don't seem to have heard of privacy round here. I mean, if we hadn't wanted to be private we could have booked the hall and had a debate, not walked all the way down to the cricket nets, couldn't we?

I thought fast. Call me Lightning. 'We were wondering if we couldn't all meet up down the beach next week,' I said. Next week was half term.

'What, a picnic?' says Marie and Carrow must have been thinking fast too, because he said, 'That's what we were wondering.'

They all said 'Great' except Mitts who said to me – she got me by the elbow and cut poor old Carrow right out – she said, 'Why'd you have to sneak off and whisper about it?'

'We were trying to decide who to ask,' said Carrow. 'You have to be careful about the social balance of things like this. Fortunately, you're all on the list,' he said.

'Carrow's got class,' Mum said.

She's right.

Robert didn't hang about after that. Carrow must have been on to him quite quickly because he came into the tuck-shop very well timed; that is, when no one was there but me. I do tuck-shop duty with Emma on Fridays and Tuesdays, but Emma was out at the back, squashing empty boxes.

He goes, 'What are you doing after school?'

I said, 'I'm going round Mitts's with some of the others.'

At least he had the sense not to ask if he could come

too, because if there was an Olympic medal for jumping to conclusions, our year would win it every time.

'You going up there with the others?' he says.

I said, 'No. I've got to see Fozzie (physics teacher) at four. I'll go on up on my bike.'

He said, 'I live up that way. I could sort of run into you.'

'Not all the way,' I said.

'No.' He'd worked it all out, I could see. 'I'll run into you at the gate and then I'll turn off down Wherry Drive. I live down there. I'll have a packet of cheese and onion,' he says. Wow! Sharp ears too. I never heard Mitts come in.

I went up the Street after lunch. I usually go with one of the others and really it's hard to go on your own because the whole school walks up and down the Street at lunchtime, except the licks who won't do it without a note from their parents like it says in the rules. There's nothing else to do except walk up and down Polthorpe Street and there's nothing else in Polthorpe except the estates and who'd want to walk round them? If you take it very slowly you can get all the way up the Street and back in twenty-five minutes, but even that left half an hour, so I went into the gift shop which is run by Carrow's mum. Just about everybody you meet is someone's mum, except my mum. She works in Norwich. Sensible lady.

Carrow's mum's all right. She just said, 'Hello Josephine,' and left me to poke round. She knew I wouldn't nick anything, unlike the Drugs Problem. That's what he got done for, as it happens. Car batteries – in Yarmouth.

I had to buy something, just to be polite, so I thought I'd get some little red cheapo ear-studs, like lips, but really I just wanted somewhere to think.

I quite liked the look of Robert. I didn't think he'd be a laugh, like Carrow, but he was nice. He had a bit of a moustache coming.

Rat'll like that, I thought, and then I saw that the only way we could be private was for me to ask him over to ours – though not just to meet Rat. We live in Pallingham. It's not the sort of place anyone just happens to be passing through and there's only about ten kids live in the whole village, all at the little school, or the Middle. I decided I'd mention it when we accidentally ran into each other after school. Then I paid Mrs Carrow for the lips and went back down the Street. First person I run into is Mitts.

'Where've you been?' she says.

I showed her the ear-studs, which I'd put on in the shop.

She said, 'Yuk. They look like open wounds. Where'd you get them?'

'Carrow's,' I said.

She gave me a funny look and I knew she was putting two and two together which could take a long time, knowing Mitts. Calculators were invented for people like her. You hear about these enormous city comprehensives with two thousand students and nobody knows anyone else. It must be fabulous.

Emma caught us up. 'Hey,' she says, 'you know that mega-zit that Flossie's got on her chin? She thinks it's ready to squeeze. Zero hour's at twenty-five past, in the cloakroom. We're all invited.'

Like I said, it was a normal day.

At four o'clock I went along to the physics lab to see Fozzie. He wasn't in a snot or anything, he just wanted to see me about my options. He was seeing us all, one after the other, though I don't know why. It was too late to change anything. Perhaps he was doing his under-cover pastoral bit, trying to find out about our problems. If so, he didn't get anything out of me. There weren't any practices or rehearsals that evening because of half term starting, so there was no one about except the cleaners, Mrs Nicholson (Claire's mum), Mrs Hales (Karen's mum), Mrs Flower (Emma's mum), and some aunties. Also the caretaker, Mitts's dad.

They all said, 'Hello Josephine.' I smiled at everybody. If it had been winter I could have put my hood up and pretended to be someone else, but everybody knows me, even from the back. I thought I might let the henna grow out, after that. I got my bike out of the shed and wheeled it round the long way, past the cookery block. Doing that, I could see the gate all the way, and Robert wasn't there. I went slower and slower, but by the time I got to the gate he still wasn't in sight. I thought perhaps he'd got kept in, but it wasn't likely, with half term coming. All the teachers had whipped off sharpish when the bell went.

I didn't want to hang around the gate in case someone asked who I was waiting for, so I got on my bike and rode round the block (up Staithe Road and back past the bank) but he still wasn't there. I remembered all that hole-and-corner bit with Carrow and wondered why he'd bothered. That's the trouble round here; you can only wonder. It's not safe to ask anybody anything, so I went on to Mitts's place and we had coffee and decided about our beach party and who was coming to it. It would be nice if the weather held, but don't get any ideas. You haven't seen our beach. It's the sort of place they use for films about what life will be like after the Bomb has dropped. In winter they go inland to old RAF camps and make films about Stalags and Gulags. You'd be surprised how often Norfolk stands in for Siberia or the end of the world.

Well, in the end we fixed on Friday because a lot of people would be away at the beginning of the week because of the Bank Holiday, and Saturdays they always end up going shopping somewhere with mum. We weren't going anywhere because the University doesn't have half terms, and Mum would rather go shopping without us.

She'd been in a long while when I got back because she had no Friday afternoon lectures then. Ben was out with his friend Mark who is even smaller than he is. We call him Micro Man, though not to his face. They live in holes in the woods most of the time.

'Interesting day?' Mum said.

She doesn't ask many questions. If she did, like Mitts's mum, I wouldn't tell her anything, but she doesn't, so I do. I told her about Robert.

'You mean he stood you up?' she said. 'Bloody nerve.'

'I don't suppose he did,' I said. 'I expect one of us made a mistake.'

'Well, ring him up and find out,' she said.

I said, 'D'you think he'd mind?' and she said, 'Why should he? He's probably thinking the same about you.'

'Perhaps he'll ring instead, then,' I said.

'And that's probably just what *he's* saying,' she said. 'Go on, ring him up – or isn't it done?'

Mum doesn't care much about the done thing, but she knows I do. Still, I thought she was right this time, so I went out to the hall and looked up the number. There were quite a lot of Clarkes, but only one in Wherry Drive.

D. J. Clarke, Fuel Merchant. Office 81019. Home 81776.

I'd forgotten his dad was the coalman.

He answered the phone himself, very fast, almost as if he'd known it would be for him. He just said, 'Yes?' but I recognized his voice. It was breaking.

I said, 'What happened to you, then?'

He goes, 'Is that Yo-yo?'

I said, 'You forgot, didn't you?'

He goes, 'No! I hung about ages but you didn't come, and then Saggers and Bonk came out.'

He didn't have to say any more. I knew what had happened – he'd had to move on in case they started asking questions. Girls are meant to be gossips, but, my God! *Saggers!*

'Oh, never mind,' I said. 'Still, it's a shame,' I said. 'Shan't see you for ten days, shall I?'

I had to say that to see if he sounded sorry or not. He said, 'Oh, shan't I?' He didn't sound sorry but he seemed surprised.

'Well,' I said, 'we shan't be at school, shall we? But you could come round ours tomorrow, if you like.'

He goes, 'OK. When?'

'After lunch? Two o'clock?'

He goes, 'OK.'

'You know where I live?'

'I'll find it,' he says. 'See you.'

'What happened?' said Mum, when I went back to the living room.

'We missed each other,' I said. 'He's coming round here tomorrow afternoon.'

'Well, that's all right,' says Mum.

I saw Ben and Friend riding up the front path.

'I suppose Micro Man will be here?'

'He's coming round too,' Mum said, 'but I don't suppose he and Ben will be *here*. They've got a new den, all mod cons, overlooking a drainage ditch and down-wind of the swamp. They call it Devil's Island.

He was telling me how they put a machine-gun post out of action and wiped out the occupying forces with smoke screens and withering fire.'

All Ben's games involve massacres and withering fire. He goes to karate classes but there are fifteen fluffy toys in his bed at night and all the pictures on his walls are of little furry animals. He'd have Rat in bed with him if he could but Mum talked him out of it. She said it wouldn't be good for Rat.

Rat was on the loose when Robert came. Micro Man hadn't turned up yet so Ben was passing the time with his livestock. The other livestock is Mog, our cat, who was watching mouseholes in the garden, and Herne the Hamster, who is the world's most boring rodent. *His* aquarium is out in the hall because he hates everybody (fiercely territorial it says in the rodent book) and would probably gnaw Rat to death if he would stand still long enough. Herne used to be in the living room too, but nobody got any peace because just as the rest of us were settling down to watch telly or something, he'd wake up and go for the 10,000 metres in his exercise wheel. Hard to concentrate on anything with that row going on. The Book says that hamsters originate from Syria. Syria at night must be full of wild hamsters all belting from one end of the country to the other.

Rat can't have an exercise wheel in case he gets his tail jammed in it.

Mum let Robert in. I heard them in the hall.

'You must be Robert,' says Mum.

'Uh huh,' says Robert.

'Yo-yo's in there,' says Mum. She doesn't call me Yo-yo herself but she knows the code. Then she went back to the study where she was marking essays and Robert came in.

I said, 'Wotcher,' and he said, 'Uh huh,' and Ben said, 'You're Jason's brother, aren't you?'

I should have known he'd have a brother.

'Uh huh,' says Robert.

I said, 'D'you want coffee, then?' and he goes, 'Uh huh,' which I took to mean yes because if it didn't we'd just have to go on standing there.

'Come on in the kitchen then,' I said, and went through. I thought he was behind me but when I turned round from filling the kettle, he was still in the living room with Ben. I'd been going to say something normal, like, 'Is your little brother as big a pest as mine?' (Ben isn't a pest but you have to say it), but I couldn't really yell it, like it was important, so I plugged the kettle in and went back again.

Ben was saying, 'His kennel name's Ratcliffe Highway but we just call him Rat. He's very shy. Let him get used to you.'

They were both kneeling by the aquarium and Rat was sitting on Ben's shoulder, looking into his earhole. He's got a thing about holes, not surprisingly, being a rat.

Ben said, 'See, I put my hand on the edge of the aquarium and he runs up my arm and across my

F.H.—4

shoulders and down the other arm. It's his assault course. Sometimes he goes over my head.'

Rat rose to the occasion, ran up Ben's hair, which he wears quite long, and abseiled down the other side of his head.

Robert goes, 'Hang on,' and put his hand on Ben's shoulder. Rat ran along Robert's arm and down the front of his jacket and then panicked because he couldn't find the way back into his aquarium, dithering up and down on his hind legs and waving his hands. Perhaps that's why psychologists are so interested in rats; they're neurotic.

Just then the kettle clicked off so I went to make the coffee. When I came back Robert and Ben were lying on the floor with Ben's right foot and Robert's left hand on the edge of the aquarium, propped up on their elbows with their free arms touching, and Rat was rushing around, up one leg, over a shoulder, round a neck, down an arm, up another arm . . . I'd never seen him move so fast. He's not really built for running, he trundles, but he can stall-turn on the spot.

'Here's your coffee,' I said.

'With you in a minute,' Robert said. Rat was standing on his neck, up on his toes, like he does, and peering up his nose.

Well, Robert certainly had Rat's seal of approval, and Ben seemed to like him, but I did wonder when he'd remember that it was me he'd come to see, not Ben and Rat.

I said, 'Shall we take ours upstairs?' and Robert and Ben started unknotting themselves. I saw Micro Man coming up the path on his micro bike so I knew Ben wouldn't be around much longer.

'Don't forget to put the lid on,' I said, because next door's cat comes in sometimes and likes to go fishing in the aquarium. Mog's too lazy for that. She just sits and watches Rat through the glass and then goes to sleep like he was a boring television programme.

I took Robert up to my room. It's got posters on three walls and graffiti on the fourth, which I painted to look like thermolite blocks. (Daft, really, because underneath the plaster it *is* thermolite blocks.) The idea was that everyone who went up there would write something clever or funny, but I ended up doing most of it myself. Mum brings good ones home sometimes. She gets them from her students who pick them up on cloakroom duty during teaching practice.

I'd already arranged the room and put out my bean bag and borrowed Ben's as well. It would have been nice to flop out on the bed but my bed's a top bunk with a table underneath instead of a bottom bunk, and it's all right for flopping out on, but not till you've climbed up the ladder. You can't do anything on the spur of the moment.

We sat down and I said, 'Do you want to hear some music?'

He goes, 'Uh huh,' so I gave him the tape rack. He chose Fat Aspiration, which was a really crappy group, in fact they've probably split up by now and formed four separate crappy groups, but they'd been at Number One for three weeks so we all had their albums, and he chose Spider Bird for afters, and we drank our coffee.

Robert goes, 'Where's your dad?'

I said, 'He works in London during the week.'

Robert said, 'People think you haven't got one.'

I know that. I get tired of explaining.

Then he goes, 'But it's Saturday.'

I'd forgotten that. Then I remembered he'd flown up to Aberdeen for a conference and wouldn't be home that weekend at all. I told him, but I could see he thought I was covering up. You see what I mean about explaining?

Robert says, 'What does he do?'

I said, 'He works for Shell,' so Robert probably thought he was out on a forecourt somewhere.

He goes, 'What does your mum do?'

I said, 'She's a lecturer. What does your mum do?'

'She works in the estate agents,' says Robert. No doubt she sold us our house.

Then we finished the coffee and read the graffiti. I had to explain some of it to him. I didn't let on that Mum had had to explain it to me.

One thing about bean bags, they sort of lie down under you. We started off sitting upright and quite some way apart, but after a bit all the little lumps began to rearrange themselves and in the end they spread out and more or less joined up into one bean bag like an amoeba that's changed its mind (binary fusion), so we ended up leaning on each other without even trying, which was nice. Robert put his arm round me and we lay there – no, *reclined* – reading the graffiti. I looked at his moustache. It was only a dark smudge yet, and I bet he shaved it like mad to make it bristle. It's the same with legs, I've noticed.

Suddenly we heard Ben and Micro Man crashing about in the hall – they were either practising karate or putting Ben's bike away. I knew it must be getting on for six because we eat at half past and Mum likes Ben in well before, because he's always late. The only times he's early are when *she's* late and then she comes home and finds him sitting on the doorstep, looking deprived. Sod's Law, Mum says.

I wondered about asking Robert to stop for dinner. Mum wouldn't mind if she knew in advance, but I didn't want to ask her and then ask him and find that he couldn't stop after all. But if I *didn't* ask him to stop I'd have to throw him out and I didn't quite know how. Most of my friends know when we eat and just go away. I wished I'd sorted that out earlier.

At that moment Mum yelled up the stairs and I got up to see what she wanted. My bean bag collapsed and Robert fell over backwards and I rolled towards him. He was so surprised he kissed me. I don't think he was going to, that is, he hadn't been leading up to it.

Mum was standing at the foot of the stairs.

'What have *you* been doing?' she says. What a

question to ask. I mean, what did she think we'd been doing, even though we hadn't.

'Just talking,' I said, and she goes, 'Oh, yerse?'

'Yerse,' I said, and we grinned at each other because it didn't matter anyway. (Not like Mrs Glover. I remember what Mitts said, the first time Saggers went round hers. Her mum kept bringing them drinks every ten minutes and bowls of trail mix.)

'Does Robert want to stay to dinner?' says Mum.

I had one of my flashes of quick thinking. If he did stay to dinner he'd probably stay for the rest of the evening too, which was nice because I'd decided I liked him, but then I'd have to find a way to ask him to go later on. I went back up and said, 'Is your mum expecting you home for tea or anything?' He said 'Yes. I'd better be going soon,' which would have been fine only I suddenly thought it was a pity and said, 'You could come back for a bit this evening.'

He goes, 'All right,' and we went downstairs.

Mum was still in the hall.

'Going or staying?' she says.

'Uh huh,' says Robert.

I go, 'He's got to get home but he's coming back later.'

'Fair enough,' said Mum and went through to the kitchen. I helped Robert get his bike out of the bushes and rode to the end of the lane with him. Ben came out of the cow parsley and raced us on foot. He won, too, because when we overtook him he fell over and made like he was seriously injured. Robert went back to help him before I could tell him not to bother, and Ben leaped up and belted to the signpost at the corner. Robert thought that was really funny. I'd seen it all before. Pratfalls are Ben's speciality.

I beat Ben up a bit – in a friendly way because of the karate – and went back to lay the table.

'Doesn't say a lot, does he?' Mum said.

I said, 'His voice is breaking. He's nice, though, isn't he?'

'Oh, sure,' says Mum. I know she likes people who *talk*, but she could have been a bit more enthusiastic, I thought.

Or pretended to be.

Robert came back at half past seven. I was out in the garden cleaning my bike when he arrived, so we sat under the ash tree and talked. After a bit things started falling on us and when I looked up I saw that Ben was in the ash tree, not spying or anything, he was just there. I don't suppose he'd even noticed us, he'd probably just stormed it with hand grenades, withering fire, etc., and was fighting off reinforcements with his back to the trunk.

I said, 'Can't you go and win the war somewhere else?' and he came down his rope on the other side of the trunk, firing from the hip and making explosive noises. Robert jumped up and chased him away, at least, I thought he was chasing him away, but they disappeared into the cow parsley on the other side of the lane and didn't come back.

I saw Mum upstairs, leaning out of the bedroom window and looking a bit surprised, so I went across the lane to see what was going on. Robert and Ben had gone over the bank into the sugar-beet field and were doing Thai kick boxing. You'd think they'd know better than to do that in young crops.

'Come on out of that,' I said to Ben. 'Charlie'll do his nut if you trample his beet.' I had to help them both back up the bank and they went on sparring so I joined in. We were chasing up and down the lane till it was nearly dark. It was good fun – but not quite what I was expecting.

Robert's family are the sort that do things on Bank Holidays – all together, I mean, not like us – so I didn't see him again until Tuesday. He came round after lunch and we sat in my room and he drew glasses and moustaches on my posters, including Fat Aspiration. I helped him with that one.

I said, 'You can write something on my graffiti wall if you like.' I thought he might do ROBERT 4 YO-YO but he just put NCFC OK! and drew a bird beside it.

'What's the vulture for?' I said.

'That's a canary,' he said. 'Aren't you a Canary supporter?'

I said yes, but I'm not. Our lot all support Man. United. I don't know why unless it's because Manchester's a long way off and it's a good excuse not to go to matches. If we supported Norwich we'd *have* to go. I can't think of anything worse than going to a football match.

It was still only half past four.

I said, 'Shall we go for a bike ride?'

'Uh huh,' he says. 'Let's go to the beach,' so then I told him about the beach party we were going to have on Friday. It had become the event of the season, the way people went on about it, and yet it had started off as that lie I told when old Carrow was sounding me out about Robert. It was all Robert's doing, in a way, so I thought he ought to come.

'Do you want to?' I said and I hoped he would because then I could just turn up with him and not have to *tell* everybody that I was going with him or worse still, have them tell me. I remember Lisa told just about the whole year when she started going with Paul Isles and then he gave her the push at the disco and went home with Karen Hales. She was crying all next day (they ought to have discos on Fridays so that people have the weekend to get over them) and we had to take turns in the cloakroom to let her cry on us. It was awful.

And boring.

Robert goes, 'OK. I think so. Yes,' and we went down to get our bikes.

Ben was in the hall, just putting the phone down.

'Micro Man again?' I said.

Ben goes, 'He was supposed to be coming over but his mum's taking him to Yarmouth, shopping.'

I knew that Ben didn't mind a bit and would ring up

someone else or go and zap the enemy on his own quite happily, but Robert was sorry for him. He goes, 'D'you want to come with us, then?' and gets him in a head-lock. Ben hooked his foot round Robert's ankle, dead expert, and they both fell over.

'Yeah, I'll come,' says Ben, like he was doing us a big favour.

Mum was just home from Norwich. She came out of the study, to see what the row was about, I expect.

'Going out?' she says.

'We're going to the beach,' says Ben.

Mum looked a bit surprised again and said, 'What, all of you?'

'Must say goodbye to Rat,' says Robert, so him and Ben went into the living room and got Rat out to say goodbye, which took another ten minutes. I went back upstairs and changed into my oldest jeans and tattiest top because it looked like it was going to be a rough afternoon.

The nearest beach to us is Tokesby, which is where people on holiday go. It's been developed — as far as anything gets developed round here. There's a concrete pub and a concrete café and an amusement arcade, that is, a shop with a fruit machine at the back. We don't go there much. The best place is further up the coast towards Happing, at Eccles. There used to be a village there but that's all fallen into the sea and there's nothing left but bits of brickwork poking out of the sand. That was where we went that day — me and Robert and Ben.

It was sunny, and quiet like it always is there. We left our bikes on top of the Marrams and went down onto the sand. There was no one about and the sea was smooth. It would have been lovely if it had just been us. We could have laid in the Marrams, among the grass and never mind about the adders, they only bite tourists, just looking at the sky and that, but Ben went down to the beach on his back, waving his bicycle pump. I knew why he'd taken the pump. As soon as he landed he went off zigzagging across the sand, bent double, and flung himself down behind one of the broken brick walls, firing the pump over the top of it.

I was just saying, 'Well, he's happy. Let him get on with it,' when Robert picked up a bit of driftwood and ducked down behind a breakwater, kerpow kerpow kerpow. I could see that we weren't going to get any lying down done for a bit and I couldn't just stand there, so I went beach-combing. I believe the best tide wrack is on the Atlantic coast. We're on the North Sea and all we ever get washed up is plastic and dead seals. I found one of those (but didn't say anything in case Ben wanted to do something with it) and a Fairy Liquid bottle that still had its squirt on. I filled it with water and went back to the others, who were still yeeowing and kerpowing, and let fly.

Ben yelled, 'She's got a flame-thrower!' and threw a hand grenade (dead crab), but Robert was the nearest and he was the one I hit. He sprang out from his trench and knocked me flat and we rolled over and over on the sand.

Robert ended up on top being bigger (slightly) and pinned my arms down by the wrists and said, 'D'you give in? D'you give in?'

I said yes, and closed my eyes because his face was right by mine – I could see every whisker in his moustache – and then Ben came running up and jumped on top of *him*. Robert turned over to fight him off and they started wrestling. Robert forgot that I was still underneath. It was how I imagine it feels being trampled by stampeding cattle.

When they had finished bashing each other's brains out we sat around for a bit, chucking stones at other stones, ones we'd named after people we didn't like. One big grey flint called Hopgood really got pounded. Then Ben wandered off to the water-line and started playing Ducks and Drakes. I have to admit he is brilliant at it. He judges waves the way a surfer would and gets the stones skipping from one crest to the next, but on a flat sea, like this was, he can make them jump ten or twelve times. His record is fifteen.

Robert was staring at him.

'He's dead clever, your brother,' he says.

Actually, Ben is clever, but you'd never guess it from the way he goes on.

Robert goes, 'I can't even make them jump twice,' and he gets up and walks over to Ben to watch. Ben started giving him lessons, honestly, it was like James Bond down in the armoury with a new weapon, the way they were testing angles of ricochet and examining stones for defects, rejecting all but the perfect ones. Ben was explaining the right way to hold your arm and how to release the stone, even the follow-through.

There can't be many ten-year-olds who've worked out a theory of ballistics for throwing stones. There can't be many ten-year-olds who'd want to. They say the dividing line between genius and madness is thin.

'What're your plans for the day?' Mum said on Wednesday. She had evening lectures so she wouldn't be back till after eight. She'd laid out all the food in the fridge in the right order so I wouldn't make any mistakes when it came to cooking it. 'Do you want to ask whatsisname to stay to lunch?'

'Robert,' I said. 'You might remember his name.'

'Well, he's not especially memorable,' says Mum. 'But nice enough,' she said hurriedly, when I looked annoyed, and ran out to the car yelling, 'There's enough for three of you!' She didn't wait to see what my plans were, which didn't matter because I didn't have any. Ben's plans were simple – he was going down one of his holes with Micro Man later on, and just now he was cleaning out Rat again. They were having a long conversation, Ben in his ordinary voice and Rat in the high-pitched sexless voice that Ben uses when he's pretending to be a little furry animal. He sounded like Robert, to tell the truth. I wondered if Robert would be a bit more chatty when his voice finished breaking.

Robert and I hadn't made any arrangements for the day, but if Ben was going to be in the swamp it seemed like a good idea to ask him over. I did a bit of my physics assignment and then went down to make some phone calls. This was sneaky because it was peak period, which costs a fortune. Mum makes me phone after six, cheap rate, unless it's urgent, but they were only local. I wouldn't have phoned Cossey in Birkenhead, for instance.

I rang Mitts first, to talk about the beach party.

'About Friday,' I said. 'I thought we could all meet at Pallingham Church at twelve o'clock.'

You'd think that was simple enough, but Mitts can't ever do things simply.

'Can't I meet you at the beach?' she says. 'Dad'll give me a lift in his van and then I can cycle back.'

'Can't he give you a lift to the church?'

'Well, there's no point, is there?' she says, giggle giggle.

I thought there was a point. The point was we should all go together, by ourselves, on bicycles, not with Mr Glover's van all mixed up with us.

Then she says, 'What's all this about you and Carrow?'

'There's nothing with me and Carrow,' I said.

'Lisa says there is.'

'Well, there *isn't*,' I said, really snarky, because I knew the more I said no, the more she'd think yes, and while she was thinking yes about Carrow she wouldn't be thinking about Robert at all, but I wished I hadn't rung her, all the same. She does go on.

In the end I got rid of her, still gibbering about Friday, and rang Emma to see what *she* thought. She wanted us to meet at one because she had to go to Wroxham with her mum in the morning. Then Carrow rang me to suggest we met at two and had tea instead of lunch and then I rang Lisa and she said she couldn't come at all on Friday couldn't we have it on Saturday instead?

It had been a mistake to start so early in the week because it gave them all time to think. If you want to get anything done round here you have to surprise people – *Hey! Let's do it NOW!* We'd have to start all over again on Friday morning.

I rang Robert.

'D'you want to come over?' I said. 'You can stay to lunch.'

'OK,' he said. 'Is Ben there?'

'No,' I said, 'he's gone out with Micro Man.'

'Oh . . . well . . . yes, all right,' Robert said. 'When's lunch?'

'Well, I told Ben to be back here at one.'

'Where is he, then?' says Robert.

'Oh,' I said, 'down his den in the swamp, probably.'

'I'll come about one,' Robert said, and rang off.

He did come about one. I did some washing and got a salad together and then went to look out of the landing window to see if Ben was in sight. He was. He was cycling up the lane with Micro Man and Robert. Micro Man went on home – he lives out Polthorpe way – and Ben and Robert left their bikes in the front hedge. I went out.

'Where did you meet up?' I said.

'Oh, Robert came down the swamp,' said Ben. 'We've been building a redoubt. It was great.'

A redoubt.

(I thought he said Ridout at first, like our English books at the little school.) I looked it up in the dictionary, after. *Outwork or field work usually square or polygonal and without flanking defences.*

Great.

Robert said he'd ring on Thursday, but he didn't. I waited till teatime and then rang him. His mum answered. She said he was down the rec. I don't think she knew who I was.

Ben had arranged to spend Friday with a different friend who lives at Smallborough, because I was going out. Mum never makes me stay at home to look after him, she wangles someone else into doing it instead. She was going to drop him off on the way to work and pick him up when she came home.

'Have you decided what you're doing yet?' she asked me at breakfast.

'No,' I said. 'I'm going to ring round the others.' I shouldn't have said that.

'Oh, *are* you?' she said, getting in a snot. 'Then you'd better time the calls, hadn't you?'

I don't like it when she goes off to work in a bad mood, but there wasn't time to make it up before she went.

I washed up and then sat down with the phone. I'd been looking forward to that beach party but I had a nasty feeling that nothing was going to work out right after all.

I rang Carrow first, because he's the most sensible, and he said he'd ring Saggers and Bonk and Paul Isles and I said I'd ring Marie and Emma and Mitts and then he'd ring me to find out what I'd found out but before I could ring anyone Marie rang me and said she'd just rung Saggers and Saggers had said Isles had just rung *him* so it all got out of sync.

But by eleven o'clock we'd worked out that we would meet down at Eccles, not at the church, at half twelve.

So then I rang Robert. It went like this.

'Hello.'

'Who's that?'

'It's Yo-yo. What happened to you yesterday?'

'Oh . . . my cousin came over. I can't stand him.'

'I thought you were going to ring me.'

'Oh, I did. It was engaged.'

'All day?'

'Well, I wasn't ringing all day. Someone must have rung you while I was trying to ring.'

'We didn't have any phone calls yesterday. I waited till six –'

'Was that when you rang me?'

'Yes.'

'That's when I rang you.'

'But I got through. I spoke to your mum. She said you were down the rec.'

'That's where I phoned from – down the rec.'

(There is no phone box down the rec.)

'Well, never mind. I was calling about the beach party. You still coming?'

'Oh . . . yes . . . tomorrow, isn't it? I've got to go to Yarmouth with my dad.'

'It's today. We're meeting at Eccles at half twelve.'

'Oh.'

'What?'

'Oh.'

'*What?*'

'Look,' he said, 'I'm sorry.'

I said, 'What's the matter? Can't you make it?'

He said, 'Look, Yo-yo . . .'

I said, 'I'm looking.'

He said, 'Look, I think I'd better not come. I think we're getting a bit too involved I mean, look, we're seeing rather a lot of each other –'

It was awful. It was like one of those photo romances in *True Love*. I could just see him standing there with the phone in his hand, and all these silly excuses coming out in balloons.

I said, 'Whaddya mean, *involved*?' I said, 'Whaddya mean, seeing too much of each other? We've been out three times. We haven't even been *out* properly. You've come here. Ben's always been around!'

'Oh yes,' he said. 'How's Ben? Is he down the swamp?'

I've never hung up on anyone before. I hung up on Robert, though. *Wham!* I didn't hang up, I slammed down. I thought I'd bust the phone and had to dial the speaking clock to make sure it was still working.

Then I sat in the hall on the bean bag and cried. All I was glad of was, I hadn't told any of the others. They'd never let up if they knew. I couldn't bear to go to the beach party. I went and got Rat so as I'd have something warm and furry to cry over and he sat under my chin. I watched my tears running down his tail.

Then the phone rang again. I thought, it can't be. Is he ringing up to say sorry? And I saw the photo romance again with me looking hopeful and a thinks bubble coming out of my ear. As I was reaching for the receiver I was thinking, ever so fast, shall I let him say sorry or shall I hang up on him again? But it wasn't Robert after all. It was Mum, ringing from the Senior Common Room. I could hear higher educational noises in the background.

She said, 'Jo? Everything all right?'

I said, 'Yes. What did you want?'

She said, 'I just wanted to make sure you were OK. You looked a bit miserable when I left this morning.'

I couldn't help it. I started to cry again.

Mum said, 'Jo, whatever's the matter? What's happened?'

I said, 'Robert's given me the push.'

'Bloody nerve!' she said. Then she said, 'Well, I dunno. He's hardly in a position to give you the push, is he?'

I said, 'What do you mean?'

'Well,' she said, 'you only had him a few days and let's face it, he spent most of his time with Ben.'

I said, 'He came round to see me!'

Mum said, 'Yes, but he was much happier messing around with Ben, wasn't he?' I was still crying. She said, 'Darling, you're much too old for him.'

I said, 'But I'm six weeks younger.'

Mum sighed. She said, 'You can knock off eighteen months for a lad that age. You're an Older Woman as far as he's concerned. He's much better off exchanging withering fire with Ben. Can't you find yourself a Fifth Year – what the hell is that grinding noise?'

I couldn't think, for a moment, till I looked down.

I said, 'It's Rat. He's gnawing the mouthpiece.'

'I'd rather he didn't do that,' said Mum. 'Look, love, cheer up. I've got to go and lecture. Are you off to your knees-up now?'

She meant the beach party. I said, 'I don't think I want to go, any more.'

'I should go,' said Mum. 'Dry your tears on Rat and have a good time.'

So I went. I didn't have a good time, but it could have

been worse. Marie says, 'What's all this about you going out with Robert Clarke?' and all the others made interested noises like when you wave raw meat near tigers.

I said, 'I'm not going out with Clarke.'

Emma said, 'My cousin Nina's seen him going round yours *twice*.'

'Oh,' I said, 'that's not to see me. He comes to play with my little brother.'

Nice one, Yo-yo.

Nice one, Mum.

It Wasn't Me

Mum put her feet up and said, 'You'll never guess what she's got now.'

Ronda tried to guess. In her view there was very little that Chloe did not have already. 'A dishwasher?'

'I'm the dishwasher,' Mum said. 'Someone's given her a slate.'

There were slates on the roofs opposite. 'A slate?' Ronda said. 'Whatever for?'

Mum saw where she was looking. 'Not that sort. A little slate in a frame like children used to write on in school. Before they invented exercise books, I suppose,' she added.

'Exercise books are out,' Ronda said. 'It's all file paper now.'

'Geoff and Emma've got exercise books. I saw them on parents' evening. "News" it said on the cover. It was all lies, though,' Mum said. 'Chloe's got hers hanging up in the kitchen with a special pencil on a string. She says she likes the squeaking.'

Ronda was lost. 'What squeaking?'

'The slate. You can write on them with chalk, but she's got one of these pencils, specially for slates. They squeak something rotten. Set your teeth on edge.'

F.H.—5

Ronda poured the tea and passed Mum a mug. 'She doesn't draw on it, does she?'

'I wouldn't put it past her. "Oooooh, isn't this fun?" ' Ronda, who had never spoken to Chloe, had to take Mum's impersonation on trust, but it sounded just like the Chloe that she had so often described. 'No, she writes my instructions on it, you know, Tuesday, *please clean bathroom, put out dustbin, defrost fridge.* She used to have one of those wipe-clean memo boards. *That's* gone in the drawer now,' Mum said.

Ronda looked round the kitchen. There was nowhere for leaving messages but, on the other hand, there was no need to leave messages. The family came and went at regular intervals; they all knew where to find each other, and when. Chloe was a businesswoman, and travelled. Mum could go for a whole week without seeing her, their only means of communication the memo board, now the slate, that hung in Chloe's kitchen. *Take down curtains for cleaners. Make up spare bed. Unblock sink.*

The sink, Mum said, never became blocked when she was working at it, but let Chloe loose in her own kitchen and in a week it was hell's delight. Mum hated to miss even a day at Chloe's, not only because of needing the money but because of what she would have to come back to.

'We got any aspirins?' Mum said suddenly. Ronda, who had been picturing Chloe's kitchen, which she had never seen, jumped.

'You got a headache?'

'Sore throat.'

'I hope you haven't got what I've had,' Ronda said, looking in the cupboard over the sink where medicines were kept, out of the reach of Geoffrey and Emma. The gas bill fell out threateningly when she opened the door. Ronda had been off school for a week with the kind of ailment that is influenza in spring and a bug the rest of the year round. Coming at the end of October, it was a bug this time. Next week was half term. School would seem very foreign when she returned.

'I hope I haven't got *anything*,' Mum said, in a voice that was calculated to make any bug scarper, but her face was flushed and she winced as she swallowed the hot tea. Ronda climbed down from the draining board and passed over the aspirins.

'Why don't you go to bed for a bit?'

'I haven't done the shopping yet,' Mum confessed. 'I came straight home, I felt so rough. Anyway, I don't want to drop off. I'll feel much worse when I wake up again and have to go and collect the kids.'

'I can do that,' Ronda said. 'And the shopping. There's nothing we need this minute, is there?'

'You're supposed to be ill.'

'I'm better now.'

'Suppose you run into one of your teachers?'

'I'll cough hollowly,' Ronda said. 'No, I'll be back before any of our lot get out. Go on, hop into bed. D'you want a bottle?'

'Bottle of gin?'

'Hot water bottle,' Ronda said. 'Go to bed and I'll come and make a shopping list.'

Chloe, she knew, made her shopping lists on a special pad kept on the telephone table; not the telephone pad but a shopping list pad; apparently there was a difference, as the telephone table was especially for telephones, not coffee or books. Ronda wrote her list on the envelope that the gas bill had come in.

To reach the shops and the infant school, Ronda had to walk down Breaks Hill and under the railway bridge, which route, incidentally, took her past the new block where Chloe had her flat. It was convenient for Mum, who could go on to work after she had dropped Geoffrey and Emma at school, but Ronda rarely went that way because the comprehensive lay in the other direction, and there were quicker ways to get to the shops. As she went by she glanced up at the building, Rewley House. Each flat had a bay window overlooking a little balcony, but it was impossible to see in from the street, for the flats were built at an angle to the pavement. The only people who had a view of these windows were railway passengers looking out of their compartments as the trains crawled round the curve toward the signals outside the station. On the second floor Chloe, according to Mum, ate her breakfast in the bay window, staring out at the trains.

'She says she's a railway freak,' Mum had reported after the first time she caught Chloe standing at the window in her white broderie anglaise housecoat, drinking coffee and watching trains. 'She says the 8.36 is her favourite. She says she bought the place because of the view. I told her we lived behind the junction when we were kids and we couldn't get out fast enough.'

'Doesn't she mind the dirt?' Ronda had asked. 'And what about the washing?'

'They don't hang washing out on *those* balconies.'

Ronda identified Chloe's balcony by the trailing ivy that grew from a pot inside the railings. Mum had to water it during dry weather and sometimes in wet, for the balcony had a roof. When she went down to the shops the windows were unlit, but when she returned, with Geoffrey and Emma scrapping behind her, she saw the light spilling out over the ivy and the iron railings. It was only four o'clock but the evening was dull. The clocks were due to go back on Sunday. Perhaps Chloe was standing in her warm window now, drinking coffee, watching trains. She wouldn't be wearing her housecoat at teatime, of course, but how nice to be able to stand around in a housecoat anyway. How warm that flat was, Mum so often said. Chloe, Ronda suspected, had no need to hide her gas bills.

When they walked by, Emma said, as she always did, 'Mum works there.' She liked being able to point it out because she had more trouble with Dad's place of work. He drove a bus. For a long time she had assumed that all buses had Dad in them, which confused her sadly when four went past together.

Then they heard a train coming and had to run to stand under the bridge while it went over. This was the main line into London and the commuter services were stepping up for the rush hour. They waited for ten minutes under the bridge while trains earthquaked over in either direction and Ronda stood gazing up at the lamp-lit ivy. Then the light was swept aside. Chloe had drawn her curtains.

Back at their own flat the curtains were open. With the gas fire unlit the sad dull daylight made the place seem grim. Ronda lit the fire, thought of the gas bill and left Geoffrey to fill the kettle while she went across the hall to see how Mum was feeling. Mum was asleep. Ronda tiptoed out again and threatened the kids with death and worse if they woke her up.

Dad went out early on Saturday and it was Ronda who collected the post, an electricity bill with red lettering. She would have liked to poke it into the cupboard over the sink with its mate from the gas board but the red lettering suggested that it might be better left on the table where someone would see it.

Ronda hesitated. She did not want Mum to see it. Mum had stayed in bed yesterday evening and was still there now, coughing as hollowly as Ronda had threatened to do the previous afternoon. She did not go to Chloe's at the weekends, but in Ronda's opinion, if her own illness were anything to go by, she should still be in bed on Monday. Ronda doled out cornflakes to the children, made a cup of tea and took it across the hall.

'How're you feeling?'

Mum sat up and lied in her teeth.

'Much better.'

'No, you aren't,' Ronda said, sitting on the edge of the bed. 'You stay in here today.'

'What about the kids?'

'I'll take them shopping first thing. They can watch telly after that.'

'I don't know.' Mum looked fretful. 'I'll be all right in a bit.'

'Not if you get up,' Ronda said.

'I'll have to be up on Monday.'

'She won't mind if you miss a day, will she?'

'No, *she* won't mind – but you've never seen that place on a Monday morning.' Ronda had never seen it at all. 'She likes to play house over the weekend. No wonder her old man took off.'

Chloe was Mrs Vernon, divorced.

'They couldn't have seen much of each other,' Mum went on, thoughtfully. 'It must have been a couple of weeks before she noticed he'd gone.'

'You do look hot,' Ronda said.

'I feel hot,' Mum said. 'And shivery.'

'Do you want me to go in the doctor's while I'm shopping?' Ronda said. 'Ask her to come round?'

'You'd never get past the receptionist,' Mum said. 'She only lets the doctors out to sign death certificates. Anyway, you didn't have the doctor, why should I?'

Ronda could think of a number of reasons, beginning

with the fact that Mum *had* to get better quickly. Ronda could care for the kids over half term, which they had at the same time as she did, but Mum would never allow her to have any more time off from school after that. Also there was Chloe, and Chloe's money.

By Sunday lunchtime it was clear that Mum was not going to be better by tomorrow. Dad and Ronda prepared the meal and they sat glumly round the table with Geoffrey and Emma, listening to Mum cough in the bedroom. She was so shaky that Ronda had to help her walk to the bathroom. Ronda knew just how she felt.

'You'll have to take a note round,' Mum said, as Ronda tucked her in again. 'I don't suppose she'll be there.'

'Business trip?'

'No, but she often visits friends at the weekends. She's got a lot of friends,' said Mum, who hadn't.

'Shall I write it?' Ronda fetched the note-pad. Dad came in to help.

'Dear Mrs Vernon,' Mum dictated.

'I thought she liked you to call her Chloe,' Dad said.

'She does. She calls me Dianne so she says I should call her Chloe, but I don't like it,' Mum said. Mum was not chummy. 'Mrs Vernon and Mrs Sheppard's all right with me. How can I call her Chloe when I'm cleaning her oven?'

'Hasn't she got one of them that cleans itself?' Dad asked.

'Why should she? She's got me. I don't mind cleaning her oven, but not while she's there. I couldn't sit and watch someone clean mine.'

'Chance would be a fine thing,' said Dad, and went out again.

'What next?' Ronda asked.

'Oh, I don't know,' Mum said, and her voice cracked. 'You think of something. You're good at that.'

Ronda sighed. She had to write her own absence notes because Mum could never think of anything to say.

'Shall I write it from you or from me?'

Mum disappeared under the bedclothes again.

'Better from you. She knows my writing.'

Ronda went back to the kitchen and wrote, *Dear Mrs Vernon, I am sorry to have to tell you that my mother is ill and will not be able to come and clean next week. I apologize for the inconvenience. Yours sincerely, Ronda Sheppard.*

They had learned to write formal letters at school but the last part was borrowed from the insincere voice that honked from the public address system at the station when a train was delayed or cancelled.

She put on her coat, left Dad and the kids in front of the telly, and went out. A sore cold wind with drizzle in it was blowing along the walkway. Ronda ran down to street level and then kept running along the side streets to the main road and Breaks Hill, only to find that the wind, which seemed to blow every way among the buildings, was coming hard and straight up the hill from under the railway arch. She put her head down and stomped into it, hearing her footfalls thud back at her along the empty Sunday street. Although it was only mid-afternoon a lot of people had put their lights on and many of the windows in Rewley House were lit. The clocks had gone back, and British Summer Time was over.

Ronda could not tell whether Chloe's window were illuminated or not. If it had been a milder afternoon she would have lurked in the street, plucking up courage to go in, but the wind sawed at her bare ankles between the rolled-up trouser cuffs and her boots. She whipped in through the swing doors and then paused to decide on her next move. She had half expected something like a foyer, with palms and carpets and a lift, but all she found was a bare lobby with a flight of concrete steps going up. The only thing that seemed to make it different from the flats at home was the fact that no one had sprayed anything on the walls. She went up.

The ground-floor flats were entered from the street. On the first landing was a hallway with four doors leading from it. There was the grille of an entryphone beside each. She found an identical arrangement on the second floor, but the stairs had completed two or three turns on the way up and she was no longer sure which way she was heading. She prowled from door to door, looking at name-plates. Chloe Vernon's was at the end, on the left. She was about to slip her note into the brass letter flap when she heard music coming from behind the door. Chloe must be in.

Ronda withdrew the envelope from the flap. If Chloe were at home it would, after all, be more polite to deliver the message by hand. In any case, now that she was so close, Ronda very much wanted to meet Chloe. Mum had pointed her out once or twice in the street, but Ronda had retained nothing but a hurried impression of a woman in a good cloth coat, swinging in the opposite direction on the far side of the street, which was disappointing, for in Ronda's imagination, Chloe was dressed in furs. She put out her hand again and pressed the bell.

At home this would have set off hectic shrieks and a stampede of feet on lino. Chloe must have carpets in her hall – of *course* she would have carpets in her hall – and Ronda heard nothing until the entryphone whirred at her side and a voice inquired, 'Yes?'

Ronda was not good with telephones. She put her mouth close to the grille and muttered, 'Ronda Sheppard.' It seemed unlikely that anyone at the other end would be able to make anything of it. She repeated her name more loudly, but by this time the entryphone had stopped whirring and suddenly the latch was released on the other side of the door. It opened, leaving her face to face with Chloe.

They gazed at each other.

'Yes?' said Chloe again, melodiously, on three notes, like a door chime. She was not wearing a housecoat.

'Mrs Vernon?'

'Yes.'

'I'm Ronda Sheppard. I've got a note from my mum.'

Chloe stared, trying to match this information with the growl over the entryphone. Then she sparked to attention.

'Oh, Ronda! Dianne's girl. How nice to meet you. Do come in.'

Chloe stood aside and Ronda stepped past her. Things could get sticky from now on. She had not expected to be asked in. Chloe was not what she had expected, either. Ronda had been prepared, if at all, for a haughty creature with a nose built for looking down, who pretended to be friendly to inferiors, but Chloe, in a little grey woollen dress, stood no taller than she did, and seemed honestly pleased to see her.

She squeezed past Ronda and led the way into her living room.

'Ridiculously narrow,' she apologized for her hallway.

You should see ours, thought Ronda, following her.

The living room was spacious and light, and seemed all the longer for being carpeted in cream. Only someone with no children, who was out all day, would dare to lay a cream carpet. Ronda looked nervously at her boots.

Chloe followed her glance.

'Don't worry. It's awfully easy to clean.' She laughed. 'Ask . . . your mum.'

Ronda had no need to ask her mum. Mum had mentioned the carpet before. She said it was a B.

Chloe sank into a soft leather armchair, also cream, like a mousse with a spoonful scooped out, and waved Ronda to the settee. Ronda perched.

'Is something wrong?'

'Wrong?' Had she been staring?

'With Dianne – your mum. You said you had a note.'

'Oh. Oh, yes. She's got a bug.'

'Flu? Poor thing. I haven't had it for years but I remember how it feels. Is she in bed?'

If Chloe had said anything about the inconvenience of losing her cleaning woman the following week Ronda would have thrown down the note on Chloe's beautiful glass coffee table and stalked out, but Chloe was really sorry to hear that Mum was ill. Ronda could see that it had not yet dawned on Chloe that she was going to suffer too, and it was then that the idea, which had been nibbling away at the back of Ronda's mind since she began climbing the stairs, suddenly bit her.

'I think she ought to have the whole week off,' Ronda said. 'But she's worried about putting you out.'

Chloe caught on. Her smile dropped but she said gamely, 'Oh, *that* doesn't matter.'

May not matter to you, Ronda thought. She said, 'Well, look, I'm on half term, next week. Would you like me to come instead?'

Chloe looked really surprised. Ronda made sure that

it was only surprise and not alarm before she went on, 'I'd like to. And Mum doesn't want you to be put out.'

'But you can't miss your holiday,' Chloe protested. Her dark curls, rather like Ronda's own, bobbed wildly. 'Dianne said you'd been ill too.'

'Not very ill,' Ronda said. 'I'm completely better now.'

'And what about Geoffrey and Emma?'

You know everything, don't you? Ronda thought. 'Dad's on late turn, next week, and it's only mornings, isn't it? I'd come in the same time as Mum does.'

'It's very sweet of you,' Chloe began, and for a terrible moment Ronda wondered if Chloe thought that she was offering out of kindness and wouldn't want paying, but she felt that Chloe probably did not think along those lines. Mum had said often enough that she was not mean with money. Why should she be? Ronda thought, looking round the room again.

'. . . Still,' Chloe went on, 'I expect you're used to helping with housework.'

'Oh, yes.' Whatever did Mum have to complain about? The flat looked immaculate except for the Sunday papers floating on the carpet. There were no biscuits trodden into that carpet, no sweet wrappers and lolly sticks in the crevices of the cream settee, no fingermarks and kick-scuffs on the paintwork, no Lego . . .

'Well then, I'd love you to come.' Chloe's bright face darkened for a moment. 'But what does Dianne – what does your mum think?'

'She doesn't know,' Ronda said. 'I wanted to ask you first.'

'I hope she'll be pleased,' Chloe murmured, in a way that made Ronda think that perhaps Chloe knew something about Mum that she herself did not. 'Would you like a coffee before you go?'

'I'd better get back,' Ronda said, rising. She could not bear the sight of her mean black boots on the carpet a moment longer. 'They thought I just came to put a note through the door.'

'Oh – the note.' Chloe held out her hand.

'Well, you won't need it now. Anyway, it wasn't really from Mum. I wrote it.'

'Oh, I must have my note,' Chloe said, wheedlingly, and Ronda passed it over with reluctance. You could, she felt, get a bit tired of someone who put her head on one side and talked like that. She tried to remember if there were any spelling errors in the note.

Chloe got to her feet to show her out, and a bell rang. Ronda thought it must be another visitor at the entryphone, but Chloe dived through a doorway that led out of the sitting room, although not to the hall, crying 'Excuse me!' Ronda caught an awful glimpse of a kitchen that belonged to someone who did not have to clean up after herself.

'The oven timer,' explained Chloe, out of sight. 'I've got some people coming in.' The door swung to, although not soon enough to shut in a smell of scorched fat. Ronda tactfully turned her back on it just as a locomotive sounded its klaxon outside and she became aware, at last, of the famous bay window where Chloe ate her breakfast and drank her coffee and watched trains. An Inter-City went by, pelting out of London.

'I hate cooking,' Chloe confided, at her shoulder. 'I suppose you're frightfully good at it.'

'Not very,' Ronda said, puzzled. Why should she be? Chloe was not just being polite; Ronda could tell that she genuinely thought that Ronda must be a good cook, perhaps for the same reason that she supposed Ronda must be accustomed to housework. Behind Chloe, in the kitchen, as the door closed itself, she saw, on the wall, a child's slate with a pencil dangling from it on a string. Then she was out on the landing, Chloe sparkling 'Goodbye' in the doorway, and with nothing to do but go home and tell Mum.

After half an hour it became quite obvious that the only good idea had been to tell Chloe first, because it was too late to go back and explain that it had all been a mistake, and a mistake it most definitely had been.

'Why didn't you ask me?' Mum demanded from the pillow in the furious shouting whisper that was all she could manage.

'I didn't think –'

'You never think!'

'No, I mean, I didn't think of it till I got there.'

'Do you have to tell everybody everything?'

'I didn't tell her anything.'

'You didn't have to,' Mum roared, silently, as her voice gave way altogether. 'She's not stupid. She'll think we're so short I have to send my daughter out charring.'

Ronda had never thought of it as charring. *My mum's a charwoman.* No, it had never struck her like that. It sounded so old-fashioned.

'But we *are* short.'

'You don't have to advertise. What'll your dad say?'

Dad had already said plenty, not about his daughter going out charring but about having to look after the kids for the next five mornings.

'I only wanted to help,' Ronda said. Her trump card was the final demand from the LEB, but she would not play it. 'A lot of the other girls at school have jobs.'

'Not that sort of job. You're going to make something of your life.'

They had this argument regularly and Ronda could never see the point of it, since she fully intended to make something of her life anyway. Cleaning Chloe's flat for a week was not going to ruin her career prospects.

'What about your school assignments for half term?'

'I haven't got any, have I? I was away all last week.'

'You could have gone round Jasbinder's and got them.'

'But I wasn't there when we did the work, was I? Anyway,' she lied, 'Jasbinder's been away too. I saw Rukash on Friday, in Sainsbury's. Same's what I've had.'

'I can't trust you out of my sight,' Mum said, and turned her head away, too tired to continue the battle.

'D'you want a cup of tea?' Ronda said.

'No.'

Ronda went into her own bedroom and snivelled for a bit until she felt better. She had at least expected an A for initiative, at least she had done up till that moment when Chloe had said, 'I hope she'll be pleased.'

Pretty Chloe: Ronda pictured her again, in more detail now, standing by her window in the white broderie anglaise housecoat, drinking coffee, watching trains. She must be about Mum's age, thirty-five perhaps, but Ronda had noticed that she looked much more like Ronda herself, clear-skinned, unlined, black curls with no strand of grey. Mum wanted Ronda to be another Chloe Vernon, not another Dianne Sheppard.

But there was no going back on her word to Chloe. On Monday morning Ronda left home to a scattered chorus of coughs and complaints and walked briskly down Breaks Hill with Chloe's key in her coat pocket. In a carrier bag she had Mum's pink nylon overall to keep her clothes nice.

'But I was going to wear my jeans,' Ronda had said.

'You wear something decent,' Mum had ordered, rearing up from the pillow. 'Chloe has people in, sometimes.'

It had not occurred to Ronda that you might have to dress up in order to do, in someone else's home, the things you would dress down for in your own.

She clutched the key, afraid of losing it. That would be a splendid start to what promised to be an uneasy week. Chloe, Mum said, was always at home on Monday mornings. She went regularly to her office on Mondays at 9.30, leaving an hour after Mum arrived. The rest of the week she might be there, she might not, but today, for sure, she would be at her bay window, watching the trains. Ronda had instructions to let herself in and she knew that it was going to feel very strange, walking into someone else's flat while they were in it too.

She met no one on the stairs, so she had no need to account for herself. Mum had grudgingly rehearsed the procedure. She closed the door quietly, took off her coat and hung it in the hall cupboard. She expected the space inside to be filled with outdoor clothes, perhaps even Chloe's mythical fur coat, but it was obviously the broom cupboard, although it contained nothing more menial than a flash vacuum cleaner. There were several other doors leading off the hall. Suppose Chloe suddenly opened a door and came out of the loo to find Ronda gaping at her? She took the nylon overall from its bag, feeling like a shop assistant in it, and went into the kitchen. There the feeling left her.

Chloe, she recalled, had had some people in the night before. The evidence of their visit was everywhere: plates, dishes, saucepans, roasting trays stood on the working surface, the draining board, the chairs and the floor. There was an evil smell of cold burned fat, stale cigarette smoke and boiled vegetables, such as rolled through the back doorway of the Cherry Pie Dining Rooms when one of the staff came out to put something in the dustbin. Jasbinder said there were rats as big as rabbits round the back of the Cherry Pie.

No one seemed to have finished anything; every dish and plate had food stuck to it with the grimly adhesive look of something that has put down roots and intends to flourish. Ronda lifted her eyes from the heap and looked at the wall. There hung the slate, covered in Chloe's exquisite writing inscribed by the wickedly pointed slate pencil that hung underneath. The message was polite but terse:

Ronda – please wash up, clean kitchen floor, Hoover living room, sponge woodwork, HOB!!!

Well, she had said please. Ronda decided that washing up was hardly adequate for the greasy pile that surrounded her. Surely nothing short of a steam hose would shift that muck – and what was HOB? Some kind of coded salutation, perhaps, like SWALK. She was just looking round to see if it might be a thing instead, and if so what, when the door opened from the living room and Chloe's smile glittered round it.

'Oh, Ronda,' she said. 'Bang on time. Well done. How's Dianne?'

'Getting better,' Ronda said, guardedly, since Mum was doing no such thing.

'Oh good. Give her my love. This is an awful mess to leave you on your first day – still, there's not much else needs doing. It'll take you a little while to find your way about, I expect.'

'Mmm,' Ronda agreed.

'Must dash,' Chloe gasped, and whirled out again in a snow flurry of white broderie anglaise, the celebrated housecoat. She did not close the door and as Ronda cast about her for detergent and Mum's rubber gloves among the stacked crockery, she could not help but notice what Chloe was doing.

Because she must dash, and had said so, she was not sitting down to drink her coffee at the little table laid for breakfast in the bay window, but standing in her housecoat, saucer in one hand, cup in the other, not drinking, watching a train. It must be the 8.36, the one that Mum said was her favourite. How could you have a favourite train? Trains were trains, all alike. Ronda turned to the sink. At least Chloe had constant hot water. How many kettlefuls would it have taken otherwise?

Mum had told her how to wash up at Chloe's, which was not the way it was done at home where everything was bunged into the green plastic bowl and glass tumblers took their chances alongside dinner plates and the frying pan.

'Glassware first,' Mum had said, 'then silver –'

'Silver?'

'*Cutlery*, then plates. Saucepans last and keep changing the water.'

Ronda collected the glasses and silverware, which

turned out to be only stainless steel after all, clattering efficiently and hearing Chloe hurtle from room to room with soft thuds like a moth in a lampshade, as she got ready for work. By the time Ronda had scraped her way through the crockery and was wiping out the salad bowl and omelette pan with kitchen paper as per instructions ('Don't wash them for God's sake') Chloe was back at the doorway in a coat of supple burgundy leather, balancing a briefcase on one knee and trying to jam it shut. She had a box file under her arm and her shoulder-bag swung heavily, jammed with notebooks. Ronda saw that, in its way, Chloe's work was as extensive as her own.

'I'll see you tomorrow!' Chloe cried breathlessly. 'Everything all right?'

'Fine,' Ronda said, waving a fish slice. She had been going to inquire about HOB but before she had fully turned round Chloe was gone. The front door closed with a security-minded click. It had a very funny lock.

Ronda bent again to the sink. Now that the steam had cleared she could see the view that Mum looked out on every morning, a brick wall and someone else's kitchen window. Because of the sink she could not get close enough to the pane to see if the block of flats formed three sides of a square or a hollow cube. She could not even see the ground, or the sky. She abandoned that view, stripped off her rubber gloves and walked through to the living room and the bay window that overlooked the railway. It was a good thing that she did or she would have missed the next round of washing up, left over from Chloe's breakfast. As she began to clear it away a train came slowly round the bend and halted at the signals; she paused to stare. It was an Inter-City, too late to be carrying commuters, but there were many heads at the windows, bowed over newspapers. One or two looked up, perhaps at her, framed in the window behind the low balcony, but she did not hold their attention. It struck her that she was standing just as Chloe did, cup in one hand, saucer in the other, only she was wearing a pink nylon overall not a white broderie anglaise housecoat. She wondered if Mum ever stood there like that; probably not, she thought.

She gathered together the breakfast things and went back to tackle Chloe's horrid saucepans, at which point she discovered what HOB meant. The saucepans were standing on it and it was black with boiled-over gravy. Chloe did not have a stove. Her oven was up on the wall, above the working surface, but the electric rings were further along, not even part of the same unit. Ronda had seen them featured in fake kitchens, as part of shop window displays. She had never thought that people might actually buy such things. It seemed a cock-eyed arrangement.

I wonder *why* she doesn't have a dishwasher, Ronda thought, returning to the saucepans, and Mum's voice answered for both of them.

'She's got me.'

*

'How did it go?' Mum called faintly from the bedroom, when she came home. Dad was in the living room, proving noisily that looking after young children was no job for a man. Ronda hoped very much that he might have done something about lunch, but the kitchen table was littered with bits of Lego and there was no welcoming veil of steam above the stove. Ronda looked in at Mum instead.

'It was all right.'

'Get everything done?'

'Everything.' Ronda came right into the room. 'I mean, I don't see what there'll be left to do for the rest of the week.'

'Oh, don't you?' Mum allowed herself a grim smile. She must be feeling better. 'You wait till tomorrow. Suppose she has more friends in tonight?'

'She didn't say anything about that.'

'Of course she didn't. It'll all be on the slate.'

Ronda had ticked off today's items on the slate and sponged it clean when she left. She imagined it laced over again with Chloe's writing.

'Did Dad do any shopping?'

'I thought you were going to do it.'

'I was. I just asked him to get the dinner things in case I didn't have time. I came straight back.'

Mum looked at her watch.

'You mean you've been at Chloe's all this time?'

'Yes.'

'Took longer than you thought, did it?'

'I was thorough. Did Dad go out?'

'Don't ask me,' Mum said, tiredly.

He didn't then, Ronda thought. Any minute now they'd be hollering for food: Emma and Geoffrey who were behaving as if they'd been orphaned, and Dad who ought to have done something about it himself, who ought to have bought it, at least.

'I'll nip down to Spar,' Ronda said. 'Get some spaghetti rings and that.'

'Did you see Chloe?' Mum said, as she went out.

'Yes, she was watching trains.'

'Surprise, surprise,' said Mum. 'Tell you what I'd like to do – go out on that balcony one day and heave half a brick at one of those Inter-Cities, right into the restaurant car.'

'The 8.36?'

'That'd do for starters.'

Chloe was there again on Tuesday morning.

'Look at them,' she said, when she heard Ronda enter the room behind her. The 8.36 was quivering on the curve, waiting for the signal to change. 'I wonder what they're thinking. All sealed in and nowhere to go.'

'They're going to work,' Ronda said. She had just looked at the slate. *Clean fridge, clear out larder, make up spare bed. Dust.* Ronda had looked in the larder yesterday. It smelled of bread bins.

'They're not going anywhere, right now,' Chloe said. Ronda peered over her shoulder. In the train one or two of the passengers were staring out, blankly unfocused.

'Probably think they're going to be late,' Ronda said.

'I'm glad I can miss the rush hour,' Chloe said. 'That's one thing about being in management . . . I do think it's a cheek, though, holding up the express for little local trains,' she added.

Even little local people have to get to work, Ronda mouthed at her back.

'It happens almost every morning. I expect they write furious letters to the papers. "This so-called train service . . . Disgusted, Colchester." How's Dianne?'

'Better,' Ronda said, 'but I think she ought to have the rest of the week off – if that's all right?'

'Of course it's all right!' Chloe cried, spinning round, so that the broderie anglaise frothed about her. 'And you're doing splendidly,' she went on, her hand on Ronda's shoulder. 'If I hadn't seen you here I'd never have known the difference.'

She turned back to the window in her usual pose, cup in one hand, saucer in the other. Ronda slouched to the kitchen, wondering why she so much objected to Chloe's innocent hobby. Why shouldn't she watch trains while she had her breakfast?

Because no one's going to look out of the bus to watch Ronda Sheppard drink her tea in the kitchen of 17 Romney Court? she muttered at the slate. *Make up spare bed.* That meant that Chloe was expecting more company. Still, it could only be one. Ronda had cased the joint the day before, looking in all the rooms. The spare bed was a single, so tomorrow's washing up should not be anything like as bad as yesterday's.

When Chloe had left the flat and Ronda had washed up, she emptied the fridge, switched it to 'Defrost' and went to find clean sheets in Chloe's airing cupboard. This was in her bathroom, a snuggery of towels, tiles, rugs and pot plants.

The linen lay in laundered stacks, no human hand could have squared them up and pressed them so accurately, and between each sheet and pillow-slip lay a sachet of lavender or *pot-pourri*. Ronda, whose own sheets smelled rather too often of a bygone fry-up, through being finished off on the kitchen radiator, leaned her face against the topmost sheet and inhaled. It smelled like the cosmetic department of an expensive store; indeed, the whole flat smelled like an expensive department store, except for the kitchen. That smelled like a kitchen. Chloe was at least human enough to do her own cooking, if not her own washing up, although if Ronda had not herself seen the greasy debris of Chloe's dinner party she would have suspected that Chloe only pretended to cook by pouring oil on the hotplate and setting fire to it.

'I'm going away this afternoon,' Chloe said at the kitchen door, on Wednesday morning. 'I won't be back till late Thursday – so I won't see you till Friday, will I?' she added, cleverly. 'Still, it's all on the slate. How's Dianne?'

'Much better,' Ronda said. She would have gone into details – she was sure that Chloe's look of sympathetic interest was genuine – but then she noticed that Chloe was not alone. Sitting at the table in the bay window was a woman, eating toast and smoking. Ronda continued to stack crockery more quietly when Chloe went back to her breakfast, hoping that Chloe would let slip some insulting remark about Ronda or Mum – something that would give substance to the insubstantial grievance that Mum and Ronda shared. Chloe got up their noses. They had puzzled over it last night because they could not decide why. It couldn't only be because Chloe left messages for them on a slate, or stood in the window wearing white, watching trains.

Chloe, she had noticed, was not wearing white this morning. She was already dressed and the housecoat was nowhere to be seen. Across the hall, in the spare room, where the door stood open, a strange nightdress lay across the bed, empty sleeves hanging to the floor, a murdered headless handless corpse. The woman at the breakfast table must be the one for whom Ronda had made up the bed yesterday. A friend, presumably.

A close friend? Ronda listened for indiscretions.

'Who's that?' said the friend.

'Dianne's daughter. You know Dianne – she does my cleaning. She's got the flu, so Ronda's stepping in.'

If Chloe had said, 'Dianne's my daily', or 'Dianne's my treasure', or 'She's my little woman from round the corner', as people did on the telly, Ronda would have stalked with silent disdain into the living room, peeled off her red rubber gloves and dashed them to the ground before leaving the flat for ever, but Chloe did not make remarks like that – fortunately. Ronda could imagine what Mum would say if she walked out. Chloe just said, 'You know Dianne. She does my cleaning.'

'I wish someone would do *my* cleaning,' said Friend.

'You could find somebody, surely? There must be someone in the village who'd be glad of the work.'

'Not from me,' Friend said. She sounded embarrassed. 'They're all my friends, sort of. Well, their kids are my kids' friends. I wouldn't have the nerve to ask.'

'Who needs nerve?' Chloe, roused, actually turned her back on the railway. 'That's the trouble, you think housework's demeaning so you're afraid to ask anyone to do it for you. Dianne's my friend, that's all. I do my work, she does hers – it just happens that her work is cleaning my flat. I'm simply paying her to do something I don't have time to do myself. I pay a secretary to type my letters and she doesn't feel humiliated. That's the trouble with people like you,' said Chloe, 'you make housework insulting by treating it like an insult. You've lowered its value. Women are ashamed to call themselves housewives these days.'

'No, I'm just ashamed to let anyone see my house,' said Friend. 'What do you mean, Dianne's a friend? Where did you meet her, in the Directors' Dining Room?'

Got it in one, thought Ronda. The only place where Mum and Chloe were likely to meet was in Sainsbury's, the great leveller.

Chloe and Friend departed in a rush, among cries of 'Oh-God-is-that-the-time-why-didn't-you-say-oh-God!' and they raced out giggling like school kids. In the empty flat Ronda turned to inspect the slate with its ingratiating message. *Dear Ronda* . . .

Dear Ronda? said Ronda. Crawl crawl. *Strip and change beds, put out sheets for laundry, clean windows, inside only, clean bathroom, hoover throughout, empty vases* . . .

Ronda made rapid calculations. There was one window in each room: seven, and all enormous except for the ones in the loo and bathroom and they were just large, but the great glass bay in the living room made up for them. Inside only. I should think so, Ronda said. The rest of the two days' instructions, crowded into the slate's wooden frame, faded beside the prospect of the window cleaning, until she saw that they had overflowed onto a sheet of paper tucked into the frame.

. . . *spilt coffee on housecoat. Left soaking. Could you rinse and drip dry?*

The housecoat, grey and sullen, in a soapy solution with all the bubbles burst, was waiting in a bucket in the bathroom. Ronda ran hot water into the bath, added fresh soap flakes and spread the garment in it at full length. Filmy rainbows glazed the holes in the broderie anglaise, making tiny windows.

Like laying out a corpse, said Ronda, who had never laid out a corpse, and thought of Friend's nightdress, headless on the spare bed. In the suds the housecoat was rejuvenated; the frills opened out like the Japanese water flowers that had come in crackers last Christmas. Ronda leaned over the bath, squeezed and teased until all was white again, and hung the housecoat on a plastic shoulder-shaped hanger from the extending clothes-line that stretched across the tub, for drying tights and delicate underclothes. Ronda had seen a row of Chloe's gauzy knickers and unbelievably, unfairly tiny bras there earlier in the week, nipped into place with miniature pegs. Everything else, such as bed linen, went to the laundry. She left the housecoat plopping discreetly onto the cream enamel of the bath and went to strip the beds.

The laundry had to be packed into a special case and delivered into the hands of the laundry man whose ETA was written on the slate. Ronda listened for the bell to ring.

Cleaning the windows took longer than expected; they were so much dirtier than she had supposed they would be. Diesel fumes, she thought, standing on the kitchen stool to reach the top of the bay window. Presumably men with ladders took care of the outside.

'Dirty, dirty,' she admonished a passing train, in the voice Mum used for Geoffrey and Emma when they picked their noses or put their elbows in the porridge. Ronda stood in the window in her pink nylon smock, leather in one hand, bucket in the other, watching trains. It was boring. In the bathroom the white broderie anglaise housecoat dripped into the bath.

It was late when she finished her morning's work, and rather than face Mum's gibes about unpaid overtime she decided to leave the bathroom until tomorrow, as Chloe would not be back that day. Perhaps she could even come in early next morning.

The more she thought about it on the way home, the more she liked the idea of coming in early – after all, Chloe would still be away. There was no chance of her floating out of the bedroom to inquire what was going on at that hour. Ronda wondered if Chloe had a second-string housecoat. Of course she had. She probably had enough for a clean one every day. Ronda had not been through the fitted wardrobes yet.

Best of all, going in early would get her out of the flat before anyone else was up: no whingeing kids underfoot, or Dad standing around half asleep and doing nothing except get in the way. Let him be the one to boil eggs, make tea and find odd socks down the back of the radiator. How could Mum have let him get like that? she thought, unfairly. Nobody could possibly be born that useless. Drive a bus? she muttered, storming up Breaks Hill. I wouldn't let him out in charge of a roller skate.

Mum was up when she let herself in, sitting in the living room with the gas fire roaring. Dim steam clung to the windows and Geoffrey kneeled on the arm of the settee, drawing dribbling slogans with his finger. He could not spell even the rudest words, she noticed. Emma had upended the Lego box all over the floor and was playing with none of it. It lay in rubble round Mum's slippers. Mum was wearing the quilted floral nylon dressing-gown that made her look old and fat.

'What are you doing up?' Ronda demanded. 'Where's Dad?'

'He had to go out,' Mum said, shiftily, 'so I said I'd get up for a bit.'

You mean, Ronda translated silently, that you were daft enough to say that you wanted to get up so he went out.

'You'd better get back to bed,' she said aloud. 'You look really rough.'

'I feel it,' Mum said. 'Get off of that arm, Geoff.' He did not move. She had probably been saying it at regular intervals for a long time.

Ronda helped Mum to her feet and guided her back to the bedroom.

'Do you want me to make the bed? I could put clean sheets on.'

'The others aren't aired yet,' Mum said. 'I asked your dad to wash them but he left them in the machine.'

'I know, I found them,' Ronda said. She had taken them out herself, that morning. 'I'll just straighten the sheets.' Chloe's sheets were by now on their way to the laundry in their special box. She had an insane impulse to nip back to Rewley House and borrow a couple of

Chloe's many lavender-scented spares. She would never notice.

No chance: Mum would have a fit. Ronda bent over the bed and pulled the underblanket straight.

When Mum was tucked in again with a cup of tea and Geoffrey and Emma were wrangling savagely over who should put the Lego away, Ronda sat down on the bed and stirred her own tea.

'I thought I'd go in early tomorrow,' she said.

'Work piling up?' Mum said.

'No, but I do take longer than you. Just thought I'd get it done early and then come away. Go round the shops and that before Dad goes to work. Chloe'll be away till tomorrow night – and don't you go getting up again till I'm back.'

'I don't get caught like that twice,' Mum said. They looked at each other and sighed.

The front door opened.

'Your dad,' said Mum.

'Well, well. Just in time to sit down for half an hour while I get the dinner,' Ronda said.

'That's enough of that,' said Mum. They looked at each other again.

When she went down Breaks Hill next morning the sky was as drab as a wet floor cloth, and if the sun was up there was no gleam of it in the east above the station.

A train passed over the railway bridge and Ronda

looked at her watch as she went into Rewley House. 7.59. She was in plenty of time for the 8.36.

The flat was warm and the housecoat was dry. It needed ironing but the perforated frills were so convoluted that the creases would never show from a distance. Ronda hung up her coat, slipped into the kitchen and filled the electric percolator, left it gulping and thudding on the hob and went into the bathroom, resolutely turning her back on the sink full of washing up that had waited reproachfully since yesterday morning.

The bathroom was the warmest place in the flat; it was like summer. Ronda took off the pink nylon overall that she had worn from home. She took off her skirt and sweater with never a shiver; she kicked off her shoes. With unhurried decision she took off all her clothes and hung them on the heated towel rail, to have them cosy when she needed them again, pausing only to look at herself in the full-length mirror. She looked nice. There were no full-length mirrors at home. The pink walls of the bathroom flushed her skin rosily. Whatever Chloe might look like dressed, undressed Ronda had to win, hands down.

She concealed her cramped and calloused toes in the deep fleece of the bath mat.

The housecoat hung from its line like a bride with no one inside. Ronda unhooked it briskly and put it on. Un-ironed it was scratchy, but the warmth of her skin began to soften it at once. She and Chloe were the same height, their hips wide, their hair black, but Chloe wore hers down and Ronda's was up. She was growing it in sympathy with Jasbinder, whose dad would not let her cut hers. She reached for the combs and grips and slides. Down it came, in dark curls.

In the kitchen the percolator gasped one last time and was silent. Ronda went back, unplugged it and poured herself coffee into Chloe's great green breakfast cup, the size of a porridge bowl, with a saucer to match. She walked into the living room, barefoot on the tender carpet, and put the cup on the table by the bay window. Then she adjusted the curtains, leaving the pane that looked towards the railway uncovered. She switched on the wall lights, and stood in the window, dressed in white, drinking coffee, watching trains.

In the distance the 8.36 Inter-City crawled up the gradient behind its locomotive and began its slow advance into the curve toward the signals. Ronda saw lights, bent heads, pale faces turned negligently in her direction. The train halted.

She raised her hands, cup in one, saucer in the other, and shrugged slightly, so that the housecoat fell back, open, from her shoulders. The faces in the train did not turn away. She took a sip of coffee, then placed the cup deliberately on the saucer and the saucer on the table. Beside the saucer, on the table, she placed her foot, bringing her whole bare leg into view. She twirled the white sash of the housecoat. The train did not move.

Ronda extended her leg like a ballerina, fluttered her hands at arms length and began an undulating dance round the table, swinging her hips and revealing as much leg as possible, all the while keeping an eye on the stationary train with its ever-increasing frieze of faces. Hands were moving, fingers pointing, but the carriages were shuddering, the train was moving on. Ronda unfastened the sash and flung the housecoat wide open, continuing to undulate until the last compartment crawled sluggishly out of view.

Then she returned to the bathroom and hung the broderie anglaise housecoat where it belonged, on the hanger above the bath. If she felt like it, later, she might even iron it, although the message had said nothing about ironing. She put on her clothes, fastened up her hair and with the pink nylon smock over all, strode into the kitchen to tackle Chloe's washing up. It looked more approachable now in the steam from the rising tide of hot clean water.

Ronda pulled on the rubber gloves. Almost she could hear Chloe at 8.36 tomorrow morning, wearing white, drinking coffee, watching trains. 'Look at them, all sealed in and nowhere to go. I wonder what they're thinking. I wonder what they're staring at . . .'

More titles in the Plus series

UNEASY MONEY
Robin F. Brancato

What would *you* do if you won a fortune? That's what happens when Mike Bronti buys a New Jersey lottery ticket to celebrate his eighteenth birthday. Suddenly, everything looks possible: gifts for his family, treats for his friends, a new car for himself – but things don't work out quite as Mike expects them to. A funny, sensitive story about everyone's favourite fantasy.

THE TRICKSTERS
Margaret Mahy

The Hamiltons gather at their holiday house for their customary celebration of midsummer Christmas in New Zealand but it is to be a Christmas they'll never forget. For the warm, chaotic family atmosphere is chilled by the unexpected arrival of three sinister brothers – the Tricksters.

THREE'S A CROWD
Jennifer Cole

How much fun can you have when your parents are away? No housework, no homework, a BIG party, and plenty of boys. Hey, who's throwing pizza around and where's Mollie disappeared to with that strange guy? (The first book in the trilogy.)

KILL-A-LOUSE WEEK AND OTHER STORIES
Susan Gregory

The new head arrives at Davenport Secondary just at the beginning of the 'Kill-a-Louse' campaign. Soon the whole school is in uproar . . .

YATESY'S RAP
Jon Blake

It was Ol's idea to play the Christmas concert. His second idea was to get a band together. A most unlikely band it turned out to be. Half of them couldn't play, most of them didn't like each other, and none of them had ever been on a stage. And then Yatesy arrived, with his reputation for being kicked out of several schools for fighting.

BREAKING GLASS
Brian Morse

When the Red Army drops its germ bomb on Leicester, the affected zone is sealed off permanently – with Darren and his sister Sally inside it. Immune to the disease which kills Sally, Darren must face alone the incomprehensible hatred of two of the few survivors trapped with him. And the haunting question is: why did Dad betray them?